ROYO COUNTY

ROBERT ROPER

ROYO COUNTY

WILLIAM MORROW & COMPANY, INC., NEW YORK 1973

PS
3568
07 R6

7/1973
Gen.

Printed in the United States of America.
Library of Congress Catalog Card Number 73-8042

ISBN 0-688-00181-5

1   2   3   4   5   77   76   75   74   73

For Susan

ROYO COUNTY

1

Well, this county is awful flat, it's wide and flat like an ocean of land. There's but one big hill, called Mount Lana, and a couple tiny hills off in the southeast corner, where we border on Yono County, which is all hills, scrub land, oak trees and straw and not much else, not good for anything but grazing and not too good for that. But our land is flat so it's easy to farm in some ways; plus the land is good, dry in a hot season but not too dusty. We get wind here but the topsoil doesn't blow away, I never did understand why; maybe because it's so flat, the land doesn't stand up to the wind. I like this county. I been here all my life, so I'm used to seeing flat.

What you see when you drive through here is farm-land, flat farmland. That's what it is, it's a farm county, except for the city over by Yono, where they have the farm college. You take any road through here, it will look the same to you; flat fields going on and on, just lots of flat fields. We grow a lot of different crops here, you've got your rice, and your sprouts, onions, beans, some corn, and whatnot, lots of different crops. You can grow most anything here, what with the good soil and the irrigation system. The state put in canals some forty years ago, dug them in all over the county and then left them to the farmers to keep up. They're big canals, some of them fifteen feet across and four or five feet deep in water. I planted golden carp in my canals one year and they got bigger than anything you ever caught in the river.

Well, that's what it's like here. Does that give you an idea? I've left out the people and the towns, but then there's not much you can say. Except for the city of Stern over by Yono it's all farm people, like myself, not very exciting people, and there are three little cross-roads towns. There's Madison down south, Yarbee in the middle and Stimson Corners up north where I live. Stimson Corners is where I was, in Jock Taub's bar having a cold one with Jock when the sheriff burst in, all in a sweat, and come up to me at the bar where I was sitting casual and calm on a stool, and says, Get your gun, Herbie Hartman, there's a killer and a raper on the loose. He was all excited. He had brought his shotgun into the bar for some reason or other, and he poked me in the leg with it once or twice, to get me stirred. But I just took a long sip and give him a close look. So he grabs my arm and starts to drag me out the door, and as we're leaving he yells over his shoulder to Jock, I advise you to lock up your women and get out your gun, Jock Taub. There's a killer and a rapist gone crazy.

Well, we went home and I got my gun and then we roared down the county road toward Yarbee in the sheriff's big Ford. It was Tuesday, it was just a Tuesday and there was no one on the road, but he had the dome light going and his flashers on front and back. He wasn't saying anything to me, just roaring along, his knuckles turning white on the wheel and the shotgun across his lap, the big black barrels pointing at me; he's got this very serious and important look on his fat face, maybe he's a little scared too, I don't know; anyway he isn't talking, so after a while I say, OK, Noodles, what's the story? Don't you call me Noodles today, he says, there's law enforcement officers from all over the state come around. That's your name, ain't it? I say. I don't have time for your shit today, Herbie Hartman, he says. All right, I say. Now what's the story? So then he tells me all about it: Luiz Merino has gone crazy, he says—you see they thought it was him from the very beginning, someone had seen him, I think, or heard him saying funny things—Luiz has gone and murdered two girls from the farm college and Betty what's-her-name, the bargirl down at Lucky's. Dicked them all, he says, and killed them. Drowned them in the irrigation ditches. Know what he did to that Betty? he says.

Of course I don't. He did a terrible thing, he says, shaking his head. Well, what? I says. But he just shakes his head.

We pulled into Yarbee and he stopped short, making a cloud of dust in front of Zinger's Oasis. There was three or four guys standing out front with their guns already; let's see, there was Freddy Cargo and Moon Cargo, and their hired man Larry. Someone else too, I think, but I can't remember who. Everyone piles in and as we're squealing off down the road Zinger runs out of his place and waves and gives us a Yahoo! Go get 'em, boys! Noodles guns the Ford up to about ninety or a hundred and then turns on his siren for good measure. Everyone's feeling good, eager and excited, poking each other and laughing. Deer season ain't open yet, is it, Sheriff? someone says. No, says Moon Cargo, but it's open season all year round on the mex.

Freddy's got a half pint which he opens and everyone takes a tad. We pass by a schoolbus and the kids stare out with their mouths open; we must have looked awful funny in that squad car with all the lights and the siren, six men squeezed together laughing with guns poking out everywhere. We run across highway nine, which is at the exact middle of our county. Someone opens a window and tosses out the empty half pint. Oh, I'm gonna get me a greaser, Larry says. You gonna have to shoot plenty fast to beat me out, says Moon. Ain't no one gonna shoot without my say-so, says Noodles. Ain't *no* one. He switches on his police radio as we're coming into Madison. By interstate eighty, the radio is saying. Suspect spotted by interstate eighty. Suspect spotted—— Noodles snaps the radio off and hangs a very sudden left onto highway five.

Now we're heading east toward the interstate, which is on the county border; everyone's quieted down a bit, you know, and is looking out a window, looking to be the first who sees Luiz. The fields here are dead flat, most of them fallow this year; they're ankle-deep in clover and yellow flowers, millions of yellow flowers, streaks of green in the yellow and yellow in the green as far as you can see. And nowhere for a man to hide; a man in those fields is like a tree in the desert.

Keep your eyes peeled, boys, says Noodles, we don't want him getting out of the county. What can we do to him? Moon Cargo wants to know. We are going to arrest that motherfucker and take him in to jail. Moon looks at Noodles and says, What? That's right, says Noodles. Shit, says Moon. Shit, says Freddy Cargo. Course he is a dangerous maniac, Noodles says. Consider him armed and dangerous. Moon says, He killed three women. Freddy says, He raped those little girls. Moon says, I seen what he done to that Betty. I seen what he done to her parts. Noodles says, Consider him armed and dangerous.

I see him! says the Cargos' Larry, pointing in a field. Ain't that him? I see him! The sheriff slows down and everybody looks; it's something, all right, something standing out in the field, but it looks more like a privy than a man. Noodles pulls off the road and we roar down through the field, through the clover and the flowers. That ain't no man, says Moon, straining to make it out. Is that a shed or is that a man? And just then we jump him, just like that, just by luck; he was hiding in the clover, lying down flat, but we nearly run him over on our way out to the shed.

Now he's running off away from us, moving mighty

fast too. The sheriff pulls in behind him but we can't go as fast as we want in the squad car, there's furrows under the clover and we're bounding up and down, falling all over each other, slapping our heads against the ceiling. Moon Cargo starts his famous giggle and pretty soon we're all just splitting our guts, wrestling and poking, trying to hold on. And there's Luiz out in front of the car, maybe fifty yards ahead now, running like a crazy steer, his arms whirling around for balance. He's heading for the interstate, which you can see about a half mile away across the field.

We're starting to gain on him now; you can see his black hair flopping around his head and his shirttail flapping in the wind. Once or twice he falls down but he's up in a second, moving again; there's sweat all down his back and he's starting to slow up a little. And pretty soon we're right up behind him, maybe ten yards away; everybody's quiet now, and smiling. Noodles is rolling down his window real slow and easy; Freddy does the same on his side of the car and pokes his head and his rifle barrel out.

Noodles sticks his head out and yells, Hey you! Luiz Merino! Stop in the name of the law, you slimy greaser! But Luiz is still moving, still pumping away; he keeps stumbling, it's more like a stagger now than a run. Noodles pulls his head back in and says, Well, OK, boys, we better fire a couple of warning shots. And then everyone is wrestling again, fighting to be near the windows, to be the one who gets to shoot. And it's Freddy Cargo who gets off the first rounds, he's in the shotgun seat; and there's someone at the right rear window, and someone at the left, and someone who's leaning over Noodles' shoulder, firing out the driver's side. But Luiz keeps staggering on; there's bullets and shot going off all around him but he won't stop. And then someone catches his arm by accident, just below the shoulder; you can see some shirt and some skin and some red fly away. But he keeps on running, he won't stop; the red stain is growing on the arm of his shirt. Then Noodles pulls out his pistol and says, Well, we better slow him down a little, boys. And so everyone starts chipping away at him, aiming for the outside of his arms and his legs.

He's starting to wear away at the edges, there's bits of him flying off all around. Still he's on his feet, no one's hit him right square; those Cargo boys can shoot, in a bouncing car or anywhere. And then all of a sudden, like a stroke of magic, he disappears; that's right, just disappears; he's gone, like a ghost, like the land opened up and ate him. And we all stop firing, we're staring but we can't believe it; the squad car rolls and bounces on and Noodles is saying, What the fuck— when whoosh! we're in the air, we're flying, we're sailing down into the deepest canal in the county, our stomachs are up in our mouths, and then wham! we hit bottom, you can hear the springs crack off and an axle break, we smack against the bottom of the canal, which is two or three inches of water and a foot or so of red mud.

And when we unscramble ourselves it turns out Freddy Cargo is unconscious with a dent in his forehead, and Noodles has busted his nose, which is streaming red. But otherwise things are OK, and we climb out of the squad car carefully, and slog around a bit in the mud, which is sucking at our shoes. And then someone discovers Luiz Merino under the bottom of the car, considerably flattened out and sunk in the mud, face down. And we try to yank him out but there's no doing it, he's stuck too good. And someone goes off for help, for a crane or a dozer or something, and the rest of us walk around in a daze for a while. And then Moon Cargo says, Well, I'll be damned, and someone whistles, Whee-oo, and then we all collapse against the banks of the canal, and we're laughing, we're all laughing, Moon is slapping his knees hard as he can, and there's tears streaming down my face, and Noodles' broken nose is turning black, and he's near to choking on his laughter and his blood.

2

When Noodles Pisco got home one August evening there was a light on in his trailer. The narrow, low-ceilinged rig stood alone in a field outside of Stimson Corners, surrounded by weeds and telephone poles. Noodles had been living there alone for almost a year, since the previous August when his wife Lilian disappeared, taking with her their six-year-old son Marcus, their joint savings ($3200), their marriage license and the German luger which Noodles' father had brought back from the World War.

He parked the squad car in the weeds and sat for a minute, looking through the windshield to the lighted trailer. The car ticked softly as the engine cooled. Noodles watched the partially curtained kitchen window and thought he saw a head pass by, a female head with straight brown hair. Lilian had brown hair; the memory shot through his huge body like an electric shock. His throat grew tight and his eyes began to burn with the thought of his wife, gone without a word, without even a curse or an argument or another man, without anything to explain her leaving. He saw the head pass by the kitchen window again and he bolted into action, throwing open the car door and striding to the trailer. He stepped inside and looked in the kitchen; a woman was standing with her back to him at the stove, boiling water.

While Noodles stared she turned to face him and smiled. She was tall and young looking, with long arms and legs. She was not his wife but she bore her a resemblance; she had the same narrow face, strong teeth and sad full mouth, and the same thin brown hair. There were long, even bangs which obscured her forehead, giving her a coy and secretive look; her eyes and her lips were made up, and she was wearing a short skirt, black net stockings and high-heeled shoes. Noodles watched her light a cigarette.

"What are you doing here?"

"Are you the sheriff?" Her voice was slow and husky, almost mannish.

"I said, what are you doing here?"

"I was sent by a friend." She smiled again at Noodles, who was looking as stern as possible; the set of his lips, tight as the zipper on a fat man's pants, made her smile weaken and disappear. "He was a friend who said you might be lonely."

"Is that so." Noodles' right hand moved slowly to the butt of his holstered pistol, as often happened when he found himself in baffling situations. He pulled the gun half out, then put it back; his hands came to rest finally on his hips. He stared at the woman, who was now looking away. The water on the stove began to bubble furiously. Noodles watched her smoke her cigarette. He set his feet about a yard apart, threw his elbows out and cocked his head slightly to one side. It was a pose he had perfected years ago, when he was in high school and so large for his age and so slow of tongue and foot that he spent hours every day glaring soundlessly at the boys who taunted him, who were half his size yet much too quick to catch and beat up.

The woman shut off the burner and poured boiling water into a cup. "You want some tea?" she asked over her shoulder, holding the pot motionless over the sink; Noodles said nothing, so with a shrug of her shoulders she poured the extra water down the drain. She looked very much at ease there in the tiny kitchen, fixing her tea; her bare brown arms moved easily and quickly here and there, pulling sugar from the cabinet and milk from the box refrigerator and mixing them together with a slow circular motion of her wrist. Noodles was vaguely annoyed by her ease in his kitchen; he felt ignored, his threatening pose was going unseen. He shifted his position, bringing his feet close together and hooking his thumbs in his black leather belt. He cleared his throat loudly.

When she failed to turn around he said, "I'm going

to ask you just one more time"; then he paused, a little too long, trying to remember the proper question; "I say, I'm going to ask you just one more time: what the hell are you doing in my trailer?"

She eased herself into the little breakfast nook by the stove, lit another cigarette and sipped her tea. "I'm here for you to fuck," she said, "if you want it. Joe Candiano sent me down. I'm a present, from him to you."

Noodles stared at her. He felt his stomach knot up painfully; it made a rumbling sound he was sure she heard at the other end of the room. "Well, shit," he said; his mouth dropped wide open, then he glared at her, then he smiled. "Well I'll be damned," he said. He discovered that he was grinning broadly; he pulled his face in tight again and fixed it in a leer. His head waggled slightly; his eyelids drooped and he winked broadly several times. But the woman was looking elsewhere, out between the flowered curtains on the window, into her teacup, at her long well-manicured fingernails.

She looked at him finally, but without any particular expression. He looked very fat to her; he was like a wall of flesh across the far end of the trailer. His khaki shirt was stretched tight across his huge trunk; he had a fat man's jiggling breasts and deposits of fat like ammo pouches on his hips. His face was really funny, she thought; it was remarkably wide and perfectly hairless, as round and smooth as a melon. He didn't look particularly cruel to her. The cruel ones were usually smaller and more alert, with quick hands and lots of talk. The little ones really liked to hurt; the fat ones did but were unaware. She looked at Noodles, who was leering at her; she stifled first a laugh and then a yawn.

"Well, what do you say, Sheriff. You are the sheriff, aren't you?" He nodded. "Because I didn't come down here to make it with any deputies or nothing." She ground out her cigarette. "Say, why don't you come over here. Come on, sit down. You aren't very friendly."

Noodles walked cautiously over and squeezed himself into the nook. The edge of the breakfast table cut deeply into his belly. She reached across the table and pressed a smooth hand against his cheek. She ran a finger along his lips. "I like you," she said. "You're very big." She smiled at him. "What's your name?"

"Leroy."

"That's nice. That's a nice name, a very unique name. Tonight my name is Lilian."

Noodles tried to leer again, but her smooth hand made him too conscious of his face. He felt fat and a little foolish, jammed between the breakfast table and the seat. He suddenly grabbed her wrist and pushed her hand away.

"Now wait just a minute," he said. He narrowed his eyes and his lips. "Who is this guy, this Mr. What's-his-name, the one who sent you?"

"He's Joe Candiano. He's from the city. Also known as Joe Candy; does that ring a bell?"

"No."

She shook her head in disbelief. "You ever been to the city?"

"Sure."

"And you are the sheriff here?"

"That's right."

She shook her head again. "Well, you'll find out. He's planning to branch out in this direction." She sat back and sighed deeply. "Hey, what do you say, Leroy? Shall we have ourselves some fun?"

"OK by me." Noodles tried to smile suggestively. "I ain't paying you a cent, you understand."

"Did I say you were? It's like I said: I'm a present, courtesy of Mr. Joe Candy. You remember that."

Noodles sat on the edge of his narrow sheetless bed and watched her undress. There were so many layers to a woman's clothing; he loved to watch them peel away like onion skin. The last naked woman he had seen was the victim of a rape/murder in April; her body had been greatly disfigured and not at all exciting to look at. But this whore was nicely made and still alive. Her slip and her stockings fell to the floor in a whispering heap. She took off her blue bikini-style panties and they were as small as a crumpled Kleenex in her hand. She stepped up beside him and pressed her breasts against his face; it took Noodles by surprise —she had stepped away before he had time to open his mouth or close his eyes. She smelled of bath powder and perfume.

She helped him off with his boots and his uniform, which she folded carefully and put away. She pulled off his extra-large boxer shorts with slow soft hands, letting her fingernails rake down the spreading dimpled flesh of his thighs. She pressed him back on the bed and took him in her mouth; Noodles gasped, then giggled hysterically, then began to pant. He came in a matter of seconds, a great flow of fluid, with a startled grunt and a painful spasmodic tightening of his behind. It had all been quite a shock. He lay down on the bed and the woman lay beside him. He could feel her calm breath against his ear.

They stayed together for a while, saying nothing and keeping still. The bed was so narrow the woman had to lie half on top of him, with her head resting against the soft cushion of his chest. But Noodles was comfortable, he hardly felt her weight at all. Her back was smooth under his fingers and her hair was deliciously fragrant.

He missed having a woman to lie with. He liked the sex part all right, he was always up for some sex, you bet; still, it was like a big hunger for him, unpleasant and almost painful when you wanted it and then too soon over when you got it. He liked the sex part, nobody could say he didn't; but he liked the part afterwards even better, when you were just lying around, keeping warm and getting your belly stroked. That was when he could really relax. Lilian and he used to do that a lot, especially on Sundays; they would lie with their clothes off, watching the tube and eating Wheat Thin crackers. Lilian and he were made for each other. They were suited in so many ways; she loved to lie around, and she loved to drink beer and relax, and she was slow and lazy, just like him. He never could understand why she ran out on him; he had always been good to her, a faithful husband and a steady provider. It was unlike her to do something so drastic, to disappear without a trace; she was too lazy to disappear.

"You got any whiskey?"

Noodles switched on a bedside light. She was propped up on one arm; her breasts were squashed against his chest. He rolled slowly out of the bed and fetched the half-full bottle of Ten High from the kitchen cupboard. The woman took a long swallow straight from the bottle; Noodles watched her throat working as the whiskey went down. He sat on the bed and took a large slug himself. He felt drowsy immediately, warm and thick from his mouth to his belly. She took the bottle from his hand and pulled on it again and again, till there was less than an inch in the bottom. When she pressed up against him this time she was boozy and loose, with a sweet and sticky taste to her. She maneuvered Noodles down on his back and mounted his belly like a saddle. She grabbed his breasts and slid forward and back, forward and back, the rub of her crotch setting up a tickle that had him laughing out loud. Then she was crawling up his body, slowly, until her hands were in his hair and she was sitting astride his moonface, rocking gently while his mouth worked away. In a minute she slid back down to his hips, fixed herself on him and ground and hopped, thrust and pumped with so much force that all his fat was trembling wildly, till he came like the volcano in a mountain of jelly.

She got quickly out of bed and began to dress. He watched her pull on her blue panties, her stockings and her slip; she stopped for a second, lit a cigarette, inhaled deeply and began looking for her skirt.

"Hey, what are you doing?"

"I'm getting out of here."

"Why? It's too late. You can stay here and leave in the morning."

"In that bed?"

"Sure."

She shook her head. "You'd flatten me out. Anyway I want to get back."

"Where?"

"To Sacramento."

"How you going to do that?"

"I don't know, take a bus. You could give me the squad car."

"Huh." Noodles sat up. "There ain't any buses this time of the night. Everything is shut down. There ain't even a bus station here."

"Well, shit," she said. She blew two angry streams of smoke out of her nose. "This is some place. You've got quite a hot town here, Sheriff."

He smiled up at her. "You best wait until the morning. Then I could take you down to the bus stop."

"I want to get out of here now." She was looking away from him, standing with one hand high on her hip, smoking fiercely.

"It ain't so bad here. Look," he said, sweeping his hand across the bed. "Plenty of room."

"This is the last time I do an out-of-town without my own car."

"Here," he said. "Have a drink." He poked the bottle of Ten High in her direction.

"Hey, why don't you drive me back." She took the bottle absentmindedly and held it against her leg. "You could run me up to Sacto in the squad car. You could put on the siren and we could fly up in no time. Hey, let's do it."

Noodles shook his head.

"Come on," she said.

"No."

"Come on, man. What's the matter with you?"

"No."

"What's the matter with you?" She jabbed at him with the bottle. "Afraid to put a hooker in your car? Shit." She made a hissing sound between her teeth and then drank the rest of the bourbon. She let the bottle drop to the floor, where it bounced without breaking and rolled to a stop. "Come on, fat boy," she said. "Let's go."

Noodles lay back down. He set his face grimly and stared at the ceiling.

"Come on," she said. She leaned over the bed and poked him firmly in the stomach. "Come on, fat boy. Don't just lie there. Get up. I want you to take me back. You're taking me back." She poked him again, harder. Then she balled up her fist and punched him right on the navel. Noodles continued to stare grimly at the ceiling. "Get up," she said. "I want to go back. Get your fat ass off the bed."

When he failed to move she stood back and lit another cigarette. She began to tap one foot rapidly against the floor. "You fat ass," she said. She flicked her cigarette, and the ash fell onto her tapping foot. "You fat hick." She stepped up to the bed again, cocked her arm and swung; but Noodles' huge hand was there this time, it caught her fist in the air and swallowed it.

"Watch it," he said. His face was very pink.

She pulled her hand free and stepped back. She made a disgusted face in his direction and gave him the finger. Then she turned around and stood for a minute with her back to the bed. Finally she sat down on the edge and crossed her legs.

Noodles stared at her back. There were freckles across her shoulders, many light brown freckles, and a long scar directly over her spine. Her long hair was in great disorder, twisted and knotted and curled up; it looked angry and confused and charged with energy. He wanted to say something, but he had run out of ideas. Maybe he should touch her, to make her feel comfortable; he raised his hand slowly toward her back, but she turned around, and he hid his hand quickly between his legs.

She looked at him disapprovingly for a minute. Noodles saw how puffy her eyes were, and he noticed the strong creases on either side of her mouth and the disarray of her makeup. She really looked like a whore then, but a very familiar whore. "Do I have to sit here all night?" she asked.

Noodles moved over until his back was wedged against the wall of the trailer. She took off her slip and stockings but left on her panties. She lay down on her back with her arms held close to her sides. He arranged the blanket over her. It was an old pink blanket, once fuzzy but now smooth and faded and stained. It smelled like a musty towel.

"What do you live in a dump like this for? It stinks. It's like a cage."

"It ain't a dump," he said. He looked surprised. "It's a little small but it ain't a dump." He curled up on his side, facing her. "I used to live in a house in Madison, at the other end of the county. A big old house. But I had to sell when my Lilian disappeared. She cleaned me out and didn't leave me nothing, except the house."

"Ran off with another man?"

"No. I would have known about that."

"You'd be the last one to know."

"She didn't have no other man, I'm telling you. She

didn't want another man." Noodles began to rub his stomach. His hand traveled up his chest and a finger explored his nose. He was looking away from the woman, at the blank off-white wall of the trailer. "She was a good wife, right up to the day she disappeared. Never fooled around or nothing. We had a kid, too, a boy just turned six. He disappeared too.

"I personally think they was both abducted. You see, if all she did was run off, then she wouldn't of taken the kid. The kid and I got along good, and he would of been only trouble to her if she was on a spree. And if she had run off she would of called me after a while, to explain. She was like that.

"I think she was took against her will. It happens sometimes. Then they send you a note asking for money, and when you pay they send you back a corpse. You'd be surprised, things like that happen all the time. I know all about it; you got to, if you're in law enforcement. Except somebody made a mistake when they took off Lilian and the kid, because I don't have a cent. They couldn't get nothing out of me, because I don't have it."

"Just an honest cop, huh."

"That's right." He looked at her closely. "I don't care if you believe it or not."

"Sure."

"I mean it. I never took nothing that wasn't rightly mine."

She turned her head in his direction. "Well, what about me?"

Noodles looked puzzled. His fingers were drumming against his belly, making a sound like muffled hoofbeats. "That's different," he said.

"Sure."

"It is."

"Sure," she said. "You'll see."

After a while Noodles turned off the light. They were both sleepy but uncomfortable in the narrow bed, not actually cramped but overly conscious of each other. Noodles rolled carefully onto his stomach, then onto his side, then onto his back. He could hear her quick shallow breathing; he was sure he was keeping her awake. Once his legs brushed against hers, and they both drew back quickly. But after a while he felt her hand lightly on his hip; then she was touching his arm; soon she was curled up against his chest, encircled by his arms, and her breathing became slow and deep. They both drifted into sleep.

In the morning he made poached eggs and drove her to the bus stop in Yarbee. She sat beside him in the front seat of the squad car, playing with the elaborate controls of the police radio and with the twelve-gauge shotgun which was mounted on the dash. He drove slowly down the flat two-lane highway. At ten in the morning the air was already uncomfortably hot; the endless flat fields of Royo County baked and shimmered in the dry heat. The highway was empty and Noodles was tired from his long night. He looked at the woman beside him; she looked younger today, highly overdressed for a Thursday morning in her heels and stockings and miniskirt, but bright and freshly scrubbed, with her hair still wet from the shower. She looked a lot like Lilian, he thought, as she laughed at the garbled signals coming in on the police band.

When they drove into Yarbee he was disappointed to see the bus already there, its engine running and its doors open. He stopped the car a few yards away and turned to the woman; her head was bent down, she was peering and rummaging in her large straw purse. Noodles cleared his throat loudly.

"I'd like to come up and see you some night," he said.

"Sure."

"Or you could come down here again."

"I don't know about that. I have a lot of expenses coming down here, it mounts up."

"Well," he said. He cleared his throat again. "We could work something out."

"Here it is," she said. She was fishing something out of her purse, a small object wrapped in a napkin.

"Well, where do you work, up there?"

"Here," she said. "I almost forgot. Joe Candy said to give you this." Noodles pulled away the napkin; it was the gun, the gun she had taken, the black luger.

She was getting out of the car. "You can get me at the Villa Veneto on Watt Avenue. It's one of Candy's places. Ask for me by name, sweetie." Then she was walking away. Noodles watched her go. He stared at the gun; then he looked up as she disappeared into the bus. The doors closed; the bus wheezed off for Sacramento in a cloud of dust and exhaust.

3

Rudy Miggs cracked open a tall cold Coors and handed it across to Herbie Hartman. He did the same for the three others, for Noodles Pisco and for John Train and for Armand Small, a cousin of Noodles' from the city. It was late Sunday afternoon, a good time to relax, and they were gathered on Herbie's long open porch which faced west and so provided a fine view of the setting sun. They were all dressed in clean Sunday clothes, except for Herbie, who disliked churches and saw nothing special in the Sabbath, and who had spent the day in his bean fields.

The bees in the hive at the south corner of the porch swarmed lazily, making a constant gentle sound like a small turbine. One worker strayed down the length of the long porch and then flew back and forth, in long lazy swoops, through the rich beer fumes and the spicy smell of after-shave lotion given off by Noodles' cousin from the city. The bee grew intoxicated; it collided once, harmlessly, with John Train's bald head, circled angrily in the cloud of sweat-smell around Herbie Hartman, then landed clumsily on the furry brown flank of Zeke, Herbie's hound, who was sleeping at his owner's feet.

"Your dog about to get stung," said John Train.

Herbie looked; the bee was walking in ever-widening circles, dragging its buzzing body through Zeke's stiff fur.

"Wouldn't wake him up if it did," said Rudy Miggs. "Only thing that sleeps harder than Herbie is Herbie's dog."

They all looked at Zeke, who was deep in an exciting dream. His eyes were slightly open and twitching; his forelegs moved spasmodically, as if he were running; now and then he whimpered softly, and his hide shuddered under the circling bee.

"That insect is telling a story," Herbie said.

"How's that?" said John Train.

"You see those circles. Well, he sends a message off to the other insects with those circles. See," Herbie said, pointing at a track the bee had made in Zeke's fur, "that crooked little circle means one thing, and this here big perfect circle means another. He's sending off a message to the tribe."

County Sheriff Noodles Pisco leaned his fleshy face close down to the dog and the bee. Armand Small left his rocking chair and walked over for a better look. They watched while the bee made circles, spirals, and figure-eights.

"Each one of them means something, huh," Noodles said. "Shit." He watched with his mouth open; his fat body was bent over as far as it would go, and his face was turning red. "Where'd you learn that, Herbie Hartman?"

Herbie took a long slow sip of beer. "Didn't learn it. I just know it."

Noodles sat back and the red drained from his face. "What do you mean, you just know it?"

"That's what I mean," said Herbie. "I just know it. It's something you know, being around bees for years."

"Shit," said Noodles. He drained his beer and crunched the can. " 'It's just something you know,' " he said in a mincing voice and with much wagging of his huge head. "OK, Mr. Smartass, what's he saying now?"

Herbie finished his beer and carefully set the empty can on the floor by his chair. He looked at the setting sun; it was turning orange and beginning to flatten out on the top and on the bottom. In another ten minutes it would be gone below the horizon, but there would be another hour or so of light, during which time the fleecy clouds peculiar to Royo County in the summertime would turn pink and purple, like cotton absorbing a beautiful stain. The turning of the clouds was the best part of sunsets for Herbie. He let his glance slide down to Zeke and the bee caught in his fur. The bee was tracing out a series of increasingly flat ellipses. Herbie thought of the sun.

"What's he saying, Mr. Smartass?" asked Noodles.

Herbie watched intently for a minute. His lips were moving slowly and oddly, as if he were puzzling out a passage in a difficult book. Suddenly he sat back in his chair, and his eyes returned to the setting sun.

"Well?" Noodles asked.

"He's saying," Herbie answered, "that he's about to sting someone stupid."

Noodles looked at Herbie a while and then at his cousin. Armand Small was a little man with thin blond hair, bifocals and many razor nicks on his slender neck. He was wearing a short-sleeve white shirt and a tie. "What do you think of that, cousin?" Noodles asked.

"I think it's nonsense."

"That's what it is, all right," said Noodles. He turned back to Herbie. "I'm going to prove you wrong, Mr. Smartass." With a considerable effort Noodles bent over again, so that his reddening face was just above the bee. "That insect ain't about to sting anybody; he's about to die." And with that, Noodles Pisco swallowed a gulp of air, pressed a fist hard into his own belly and shot a long loud belch, redolent of beer and of the pork tacos he had eaten eight hours earlier, directly onto the frantically circling bee. Rudy Miggs was standing nearly ten feet away, but he covered his mouth and pinched his nose shut with a quick hand, as did everyone else. Only Armand Small was somewhat slow in reacting, as he was less familiar than the rest with the power of Noodles' internal gases. The bee in Zeke's fur became absolutely still; its transparent wings and antennae seemed to shrivel; but in the convulsion of death it leaped straight up and thrust its stinger deep in Noodles' fleshy lip, then fell back on Zeke's brown fur, where it burrowed frantically and died. Noodles roared in pain and the dog shuddered violently from the tickle of the bee, but he was still asleep, Zeke remained asleep, and this is what he dreamed:

By the clear stream in the cottonwoods under the red ball of the sun were the man and the dog. The air was heavy over the green flat land and the air was full of flying things with shining wings. The man and the dog were both the color of the gravel in the stream and the color of the trees and the color of the dark earth. Down the clear stream came the sound, a nervous drone, light as the stream and heavy as the hot air, a buzz, abuzz, the sound of that, surrounding the man and the dog so they were perfectly still inside the drone, their ears and their skin vibrating inside of the sound, abuzz abuzz. Then the man bent to the edge of the stream and took the bone, bleached white bone light as air, wide and gently curved like the clear stream, and the man took the stick which was straight and heavy, black like the flat earth which was everywhere, all around, flat from here to the rim of the sky, and the man struck the bone to the stick in a slow way, aclack abuzz abuzz aclack, the stick and the bone speaking with sharp tongues inside the buzz, which was the sound of the heat and the flying things which hung in the haze over the clear stream. And then they moved out of the cottonwoods and along the stream, the brown man and the brown dog like six feet with one mind, and the man's arms made the collision that made the sound, aclack in the abuzz, aclack down the hazy stream, aclack which was the sound of the brown man, down the clear water, over the pebbles and over the large white rocks gleaming in the sun, over the thickets of cottonwood and the sage and the yucca, through the leaves of the birches trembling and dusty in the heat, aclack in abuzz out over all the flat land.

Herbie's face was drenched in sweat and he had the hiccups from laughing too hard. John Train was laughing silently, with his shiny head buried in his scarred farmer's hands, and Rudy Miggs, who was three hundred pounds and nearly seven feet tall, was laughing his odd squeal, a thin eeeeeee sound, like the wail of a young girl. Only Armand Small and Noodles didn't laugh.

Nancy Hartman heard the commotion from the kitchen and came out with a baking-soda plaster which she applied to Noodles' swelling lip. Her fingers were long and smooth and there was comfort in the briefest of her touches. Noodles closed his eyes and let his huge sun of a head roll back. The pain was terrible, shooting through his face in lightning flashes. His lip felt big and floppy, like a slab of uncooked meat. I bet I look stupid, he thought; he heard the others laughing, and he knew they were laughing at his lip. Well, I just won't go to work tomorrow, that's all, he thought; I won't have every asshole in the county laughing me down. But the lip actually looked much smaller than it felt, as Noodles would discover later that night when he examined himself in his bathroom mirror. And by Monday morning the sting would be a barely noticeable red dot, and Noodles would cruise the county as usual, scaring loafers in the Mexican section and giving a record number of speeding tickets.

Herbie opened another Coors and took three quick sips to kill his hiccups. "Well, it just goes to show you," he said. "You got to pay attention to the signs."

"That's right," said Rudy Miggs. The laughter had drained from his long face, leaving it dull and wooden once again. A fly buzzed his head and, without changing his expression or focusing his mournful brown eyes, he snared it in mid-air with one grab of a giant hand.

"Yessir," Herbie said. "Now just look there." He pointed at the bank of orange and pink and purple clouds in which the sun had set. "When a sun sets like that it means something or other about the weather. Or look there," he said, indicating the beehive at the corner of the porch. "When bees swarm so late in the day it means something particular, I don't know what. Or when a dog has a dream and it makes him twitch, you know he's giving off a sign."

"What sort of a sign?" asked Armand Small.

Herbie watched Zeke shiver and roll his half-closed eyes. "Oh, I don't know," he said. "I can't read too many signs anymore."

"Well, then it don't do you any good."

"I suppose that's true," Herbie Hartman said. He sipped his Coors. He pressed the toe of his boot softly against Zeke's recently fed belly and the dog groaned softly and time was when a brown man walked with a dog through the cottonwoods beside a clear stream in the flat country under a red sun. It was the time so long ago that men were hard to tell from the spirits taking the form of men, and everything was in its beginning. The brown men who lived in a circle of round huts and who looked at the red sun and the white full moon and who drew circles in the dirt, they were in their beginning; the flat land was in its beginning, stretching to the low round mountains here and to the high holy mountains there, dark flat land under sage and manzanita; all the animals were in their beginning, small red deer not sure they weren't dogs, brown bear and big cats from the hills, snakes who loved heat and snakes who loved water, sparrows and jays and black-birds, grouse and quail and woodcock and gray geese, red-tailed hawks and eagles and vultures with bloody beaks, bald horses and horses with fur, animals big as hills with curved tusks, fat fish and tiny fish, silver, gold, blood red, brown, spotted, streaked, rainbowed, and monsters that took any form, men with one eye and fangs, lizards with fur and withered breasts, cats that caused rain when they growled, or split the sky with their shrieks, and the giant hairy men without necks who ate berries, the bigfoot, the yeti. The flat land was full of beings.

The man and the dog made their way along the creek. The man made his sound with a bone and a stick, aclack inside the buzz of the things in the hazy air. As the red sun went down they entered the circle of the village and the man sat down with the others. They ate from the red basket, passing it around the circle, taking fish and red meat warmed in the fire, blackberries, grubs, bear fat, cakes made out of crushed roots, greens and lilies from the creek. Then they ate holy plants from the beautiful Pomo basket, which was woven out of weeds and straw dyed blue, yellow, red and black.

Then the oldest man sat at the top of the circle, facing the last glow of the sun, and he held up a bone and a stick and he made them aclack, and for the first time he pronounced the name of the place, Oyo; he pronounced the name of the people, Nis; and he gave the names for everything else, the mountains here and there, each bird, each fish, each bug, each beast, the river with the white rocks, the narrow creek, each tree, each plant, everything he had noticed so far. The men in the circle repeated the names together; some of them fell asleep from all the food, others got up and danced heavily, in slow circles; the naming went on until everything had been given a word.

Then the old man made aclack with a bone and a stick, and the sleepers woke up and the dancers stopped, and everyone looked at the old man's round brown face, which was creased like a valley full of rivers. And he said his vision: the Nis were alive in the fullest time of the world, when everything was both perfectly new and perfectly ripe. The world was perfect, all its parts were in harmony. But there had been a time before, when nothing was alive, when nothing had a form, because nothing existed, and the world was deader than a burned-up bone. Then the world came alive; but there would be a time, longer ahead than they could think of, but not longer ahead than he, the old man, could dream of, when the world would be a burned-up bone again, formless and black, empty and not there; when everything would be dead, when nothing would be left, not even a single man to remember it, or the soul of a man, or a single spirit, or the mind of a dog. And when the people in the circle heard this vision they wailed in fear, thinking how dead the world would be. But the old man made aclack, and spit in the fire; he belched and farted and ordered more food; it was not the time to wail, he said, because the future was too far away even to think of; now was the fullest time; it was a night to eat and dance. So everyone ate some more and danced in endless circles, and laughed till they thought their hearts would crack in two.

Nancy Hartman slammed shut the oven in the kitchen. It was her signal, which everybody recognized; it was time her husband came to dinner. Rudy Miggs and John Train stood up. John's arthritic legs ached from sitting too long and Rudy had to unbuckle his belt over his beer-swelled stomach. They walked to Rudy's old black Oldsmobile.

The bees at the corner of the porch continued to swarm. Armand Small got up and shook Herbie's hand. He had a wide friendly smile. "The sheriff tells me you've got acreage for sale," he said.

"That's right."

"Whereabouts?"

"Down around Yarbee, in the center of the county. On either side of Rock Creek."

"Well, I might be interested," said Armand Small. "I'll be up for the week, and maybe we can talk business."

Herbie smiled and nodded. "Noodles didn't say you wanted to farm."

"I'm not a farmer, I'm in real estate. We're going to subdivide."

Herbie chuckled softly. "You can't build houses on that land," he said. "Nobody's lived down there for five hundred years, I bet. It's just too damn hot. And there's millions of mosquitoes come out of the creek at night; they're thick as clouds. You'd have to be crazy to buy a house down there."

"Maybe so," said Armand Small, peering shrewdly over his bifocals, "but then there's a lot of crazy people. Things are changing. You just wait; in ten years you won't recognize a thing about this little county."

"I won't, huh," said Herbie Hartman. He yawned.

Noodles stood up noisily and stretched. His lip ached considerably less but still it occupied all of his attention. The sound of his chair scraping against the wooden porch woke Zeke, who followed Noodles and his cousin to the squad car and barked hoarsely as they bounced off down the drive.

4

Bokaw was a farmer who sold hay, alfalfa or oat, and who would board your horses for you through the winter in the rotted second barn he called a stable. He lived all alone on the only high ground in Royo County —Mount Lana, which was named for his wife, dead these forty years. She was a great beauty, born Lana Treegood in Madison, where her people still live though they've fallen on hard times. I have seen an old photo or two of her in the Treegood house, which is more of a shack now; she was a great beauty, there's no doubting it, a blonde with ruby lips and big dark eyes that just burn into you, even out of a picture so old it is crumbling into flakes. The story is that Bokaw killed two men to marry her, and then moved up on that mountain, which didn't have a name yet, so he could see his enemies coming from afar off. He built a small cabin and they lived there for a year until she passed away in the terrible winter of 1932, with an unborn child in her. I don't know the truth, since I had only just been born; they say she was found in the snow, half eaten away by prairie dogs. Now they call it Mount Lana. Bokaw built himself a farm and lived up there alone.

Some said he was a good man and others called him a devil. He didn't take to people, any people, though he had a magic hand with the animals. He cured the old way, with medicines he made himself and without any use of the knife. If you boarded a sick horse with him, you'd get back a healthy animal with a silky coat and strong legs; if you wanted, he would feed your chickens herbs and other things that made them lay like crazy, though sometimes the older hens died from all the excitement. Once Armand Pisco had a prize bull he got in Texas that was refusing to hold up his end in the stud business, and he showed him to all the certified vets around but they were stumped; they tried this, they tried that, they even did an operation on his equipment, which was right impressive to the eye; nothing worked a bit. Until they hauled him up the mountain, and let Bokaw feed him one of his secret mixes. The bull got a sudden wild look in his eyes, shook his horns and snorted like a locomotive, and tried to mount a sawhorse that was handy, and tried to mount Armand when he stepped inside the pen, and tried to mount the pickup truck as they were loading him in, tripping over his own organ that had suddenly come awake. When they got him to the flatlands he did as had been hoped he would; even broke the back of the first heifer they served him, which cost Armand a pretty penny.

Yes, Bokaw had a hand with animals. Dogs were the only animals he didn't like; he was known to shoot a dog or two that wandered on his place. His house was full of cats, dozens of cats of all colors and sizes that would lay around all day and then rush into the kitchen like a stampede to get their dinner. Bokaw would always accept a litter of kittens that nobody else wanted. You had to say he loved cats; though there were some who said he did experiments on them, grafting extra heads and organs on, or seeing how long they could live without a skin, or seeing what some new herb concoction would do to them. But then everybody told wild stories about Bokaw. My own daughter Pearl says that Bokaw kept himself alive on fried cat; her teacher told her that in school. Maybe he did, maybe he didn't. People will say anything about a man who lives alone on a hill.

He was a peculiar sort of character, though; there was his looks, for a start. He had a great round head with a point on it, a real point, and wiry white hair that sprouted from the point in all directions. He had one bad eye that had lost its center and gone cloudy, like a jelly candy; the other one was sky blue and bulged out a ways. He was a big man, too, well over six feet with a lot of meat on his bones, with big red hands he would use like baling hooks when he was loading up some hay you had bought off him. Little kids and dogs couldn't stand to look him in the face. He never got false teeth when his real ones fell out and he never bothered with a patch for that eye. And in the later years his face got to look pretty awful, with lots of age spots and ruptured veins in the skin, and a disease from the sun that made big scaly pieces flake off. There was one woman went crazy because of that face. She had a sickly baby a few months old that she was in the habit of leaving on the front porch to nap in the afternoons. One day she heard the baby crying and went out on the porch and found old Bokaw with his face down in the cradle, fixing his good eye on the kid. The woman grabbed the baby in her arms, looked at Bokaw and ran off screaming into the house. Well, that night the baby took sick with rheumatic fever, and in a day or two it was dead. The woman just cracked; she ran around town screaming about Bokaw's face, and how he cursed her baby with it, and gave her baby the evil eye. They have her locked up in the hospital by Sonoma now; but the people in town believed her, they believed old Bokaw worked a spell on that child.

There was other strange occurrences in this county that it was claimed Bokaw had a hand in. E. C. Taub called him down once to give a treatment to his chickens, who had slowed their laying down to almost nothing. Well, Bokaw fed them his wild greens and such, and they began to lay like prize-winners, as was expected. But one morning E.C. was making eggs for breakfast, and when he cracked them open they was

full of blood, all of them; not just a speck of blood—
all blood, no yolk and no white, just dark blood. When
that cleared up they tried to raise some chicks, but all
they could hatch was freaks: some birds without heads,
and some without wings, and some with legs that looked
like flippers or even hands.

Then the Hoffmann ranch called Bokaw in to doctor
a bunch of sick cows. They started pouring out milk
again, but it would turn dark and salty in the pail, until
it was no good to drink. Also a couple of the cows went
blind, and another one ate the head off a calf she had
just dropped. Hoffmann tried to get the law after Bokaw
when that happened, but Noodles Pisco, who is the
sheriff since Martin Zinger passed away, Noodles
couldn't figure out what to charge him with; he never
called himself a doctor or a vet, so it wasn't a case of
fraud; he never signed a bill or took anything but cash,
so there was nothing to show against him in court; and
if it was sorcery, which is what Hoffmann claimed, then
there was nothing to do for it, because Noodles couldn't
find it in the book of crimes.

Other things happened. Ben Seaman from Yono
County had a mess of pigs who got condemned because of the trichina, but he had heard of Bokaw's
miracles so he thought he would give him a try. Well,
Bokaw puzzled it out for a while; he had never worked
on pigs before, and the trichina is supposed to be
uncurable anyway; he finally hit on a combination treatment, natural vitamins plus a special grain plus a green-
ish powder whose contents he would not reveal. They
fed the treatment to the pigs for a week and then they
ran a test, and damn if their meat wasn't pure and

clean. Well, of course Ben Seaman was pleased, and he butchered his pigs right off and sold them to the packer. He saved one old hog for his annual porkfest, when he feeds all his relatives and his neighbors, and they hung the carcass up on a spit and put it to the fire. But as it cooked the meat turned black, and then sort of blue, and finally sort of green, dark green, and it gave off the worst smell, the smell of something dead too long. And Moon Cargo from Stimson Corners ate some on a dare, just the tiniest piece; it knocked him down with terrible cramps in his belly, and they rushed him to the hospital in Stern to put a pump down his throat.

Then last fall a woman from Madison gave birth to a girl child without a face. That's right, no face; just a blank sheet of skin on the front of her head. It was a terrible thing to see, I've been told; it made you want to cry, and put your hands on your own face, to keep it there. Well, old Bokaw hadn't been in town for months when it happened, but the woman claimed she had seen him in a dream some few days before the birth, and he was wearing horns and breathing fire out of his toothless mouth, and shaking a forked stick at her full belly, and poking it into her private area. She told her dream to everyone, and then when the child died, which was a blessing from God, she made a wild scene at the funeral. She screamed out Bokaw's name and called him the devil, and said she would put him in his grave herself if there was no man with the backbone to right the terrible wrong she had suffered, etc. etc. I happened to be at the service, though the people weren't kin of mine; I just like a funeral now and again, to calm me down. But it was the most unpeaceful funeral I've ever been at; the men were struck right in their pride by that woman's words, and they had to take her away gasping and sobbing, and then they turned to each other and glared and muttered and looked murderous, and someone faced about and spit in the direction of Mount Lana, which you could see four or five miles away, rising straight up out of the flat fields.

Early in November old Bokaw came down to Madison to get some supplies and visit the Treegood family. We found out later it was Bokaw had been keeping the Treegoods alive through all their troubles, with money from his animal cures and his hay business. Well, Lucille Ravenswood of Yarbee had to pick that very day to birth a set of twins that was joined at the hip and at the shoulder. They rushed them to the hospital in Stern and had a team of university doctors work them over day and night, but they could only save the one child, a boy, and his arm and his leg didn't come out quite as good as they hoped. Of course, everybody connected Bokaw up with this latest business, and they recalled the baby without a face, and Ben Seaman's hog, and the cows whose milk turned dark, and the eggs that was full of blood. Tempers all over the county got out of hand, and people started making plans.

Noodles Pisco was visiting over at my place that afternoon. He was off duty but he had his uniform on; only thing he likes better than his uniform is the siren on his car. We were sitting on the porch having a beer, and Noodles was telling me all about the brace of monster shotguns he had got and was going to mount on his dashboard, just like the Highway Patrol; up comes young Johnny Treegood in their old pickup, out of breath and shaking with fear, with the news that the mob has old Bokaw holed up in the Treegood house, and they're threatening to burn him out, and half of them have got their guns, and the other half are carrying lynch ropes. Well, Noodles' mouth dropped open; you could see he wished that uniform would vanish off his back; he couldn't get a word out for a minute or two, and when he did he sounded like he was about to strangle. He looked to me like I might tell him he didn't have to go, but I kept my mouth shut; Johnny Treegood stood there looking at us, panting hard and making his hands into fists.

So we drove down to Madison with the boy, and we came on the crowd as they were tossing stones through the windows and trying to start a torch. They calmed down a bit when they saw Noodles, I don't know why; they sort of cleared away and we walked right up to the front, where Carl Ravenswood and his three sons were, carrying plenty of rope and enough firepower to win a war. But we marched right by and up to the front door, which the Treegoods unlocked, and Noodles disappeared inside. Then he came out with old Bokaw behind him; I hadn't seen him in a year, and it was a shock how he had aged. He had lost all the hair from the point on his head and his face looked like a checkerboard, and the flesh hung loose on him like wet clothes, as happens to a large man when he gets on. But he didn't look afraid; he stood right up with Noodles as he walked him toward the squad car through the crowd.

They were nearly there when a gun went off and

caught Bokaw in the leg; there were a couple more shots, and I saw a Ravenswood lay a two-by-four hard against his head. But Bokaw didn't drop; in fact he shot off like a young horse and made it to Johnny Treegood's pickup and roared off down the road. The crowd was too surprised to get off more than a couple of late shots, and when some of them finally made like they were going to chase, Noodles hopped up on the hood of the squad car, fired off his pistol three times and announced that the whole mob was under arrest. It stopped them cold, long enough for Bokaw to get gone.

Well, that was on Friday. On Saturday the Ravenswoods drove up Mount Lana in broad daylight, stood in front of Bokaw's house and ordered him to surrender. They got blasted in front with birdshot for their trouble; one of the boys caught it full in the face, and they had to tear down the mountain to get him to a doctor that would save his eyes. Carl Ravenswood was plenty mad now, and he swore he would make old Bokaw burn. All day Sunday he rode around the county firing people up to get the witch, the sorcerer, the devil; it was strange talk, but people were ready to hear it. Just as the heat was developing, Noodles Pisco decided he needed a vacation, and he took off for the Feather River to catch some trout. Noodles is like that, he doesn't thrive on trouble; he is a fat man, and fat men are quick to sweat.

So on Sunday evening I was all alone on the porch, feeding the mosquitoes and feeling good while the sun went down. Then I saw the boy come up the drive, walking slow but determined, like nothing could stop him. He came to in front of the porch and stared up at me; his hands were working into fists and his face was all white; he kept his eyes on me all the time, never even blinked, and his look felt like a burn on my face. Then he said "Herbie Hartman" slow and definite, like he was telling me what my real name was; he looked me in the eyes and said it once again, my name. Then I got up and went around back and started the pickup, and I drove around front and he got in and we took off for the town.

There were twenty or thirty cars and trucks parked in a line just outside of Madison on the road to Mount Lana. It looked like a funeral procession about to get under way, except that the cars were full of people laughing and shouting at each other, dogs were barking and kids running around, folks drinking beer and rough-housing and gunning their engines. A few had lit up torches which they would wave across the dark sky. I drove past just before they got under way, and no one seemed to pay me any attention; everyone looked to be having a lot of fun. I turned off my lights and we tore through the dark down highway seven, which is perfectly straight and flat. When we started to climb the mountain I looked back; the procession was on the move, maybe ten minutes behind, glowing in the dark like a giant caterpillar on fire.

At the top of the mountain there was a gate across the road, and Johnny got out to open it. I began to wonder what I was going to do. If we could convince Bokaw to leave there was an old dirt road down the backside of the mountain, which was passable once and might be still; it led into highway five, which would take us to the interstate. We had a good chance to make it, I figured; my old truck can move when it wants, and we would have a good enough jump on the mob, if they didn't take the paved road down and cut us off. I just about had Bokaw saved in my mind. Johnny swung the gate open and we drove on up to the farm.

Well, it was awful dark when we got to the house. I hopped out and couldn't see a thing, though I could hear the roar of the procession, the engines and the honking horns, not too noticeable but getting louder and louder while I listened. Then my eyes adjusted to the dark and I yelled out "Bokaw!" as loud as I could, but there wasn't any answer. So I yelled out "Bokaw!" again; and "It's friends! Johnny Treegood and Herbie Hartman! We're here to save you from the mob!" But the house was as quiet as death. Little Johnny brushed up against me; I could feel him trembling and hear his gasping breath. The crowd was getting near, you could see a faint glow from down below and the beams of headlights shooting up against the low clouds. I ran up to Bokaw's door and pounded on it; "Bokaw!" I was yelling, "there ain't much time! I've come to save you!" We heard the metal gate down at the edge of the farm snap apart as the trucks drove through it; we saw their headlights snaking up the drive. "Hurry!" Johnny whispered at me; we threw our shoulders against the door and it flew open with a crash.

I ran inside and yelled "Bokaw!" once more. It was dark and close in that house; I couldn't see a thing, but I could feel lots of furry bodies rushing past, brushing against my legs and getting caught underfoot. It was the cats, Bokaw's herd of cats; they began to shriek and moan and scratch at me when we collided. It was almost too late; light from the cars and the torches was filtering in through the open door of the house, and I could hear shouts and horns and engines coming into the yard. "I'm here to save you!" I yelled; and just then Johnny found a light switch and turned it on, and we were blinded for a second; and all the cats froze just where they were, their little eyes narrowed and blinking. And then we saw Bokaw, lying in the middle of the floor, with bullet holes in his legs and his arms and his chest; and perched around his head there were the cats, dozens of hungry cats, with the flesh still in their jaws. And we stood there and watched, neither one of us able to move; then the rocks began to crash through the windows, and dozens of torches followed them in, and we could hear the shouts of the hungry crowd outside; and we escaped just as the house exploded in flames, in hungry flames that ate it away to nothing.

5

I

On a Thursday morning late in November, in the gray
and deserted-looking town of Yarbee, in the middle of
Royo County, a late-model blue Pontiac pulled up to
the lone gas pump in front of Leo Train's general store.
A young man in unfaded overalls, with recently bar-
bered thick brown hair and a wide cleanshaven face,
strode out to the car and listened briefly to the driver's
instructions. The metallic creak of the gas cap being
unscrewed and the clank of the pump nozzle fitting into
the tank echoed down the empty, gray and dusty street,

through the cold air under a solid ceiling of gray clouds.

The young man's breath came out in white puffs that disappeared quickly in the dry air. As he leaned across the windshield of the car, scraping with his fingernail through a paper towel at the crusted body of a smashed insect, he noticed that the two men in the front seat of the Pontiac were watching him closely. They were black men, fortyish, dressed neatly in conservative dark suits; the driver had a peculiarly flat nose and many welts and scars around his small filmy eyes; the man to his right wore sunglasses and a felt hat with a feather in the brim. They watched him closely, silently, as he cleaned the windshield. He walked to the rear of the car and as he squeezed in the last few pennies of gas he saw a black hand emerge from the driver's window and a long black finger motion him forward.

"What's your name, boy?" The man with the smashed nose was looking dead ahead, over the steering wheel.

"Cecil Train."

"How's that?"

"Train."

The black man stared dead ahead; he said nothing for a moment; then he sighed loudly.

"Yeah. Well, we are looking for a friend of ours, name of—" here he paused; he reached into his vest pocket and pulled out a glossy photograph with a name printed in neat caps on the back; he looked down at the name; "a friend of ours, name of Morris Goldberg. Sometimes known as 'Buck,' Buck Goldberg."

Still looking dead ahead, he showed the photo to the young man. The face in the picture was obscured by thick curly hair and a full dark beard; two large eyes showed through the mask of hair like lights in a forest.

"We are looking," said the driver, "for this young man, for this friend of ours, cause we have got a important present for him, something he needs real bad."

The young man examined the photo and shook his head. "Don't know him."

"Take a good look."

"Still don't know him."

The driver held the photo out for a few more seconds, then slid it rapidly into his pocket.

"Well," he said, reaching forward to start the car, "you keep your eyes open. We gonna be back." Suddenly he laid a finger against his stump of a nose and looked quickly, searchingly, into the young man's face. "What you say your name was?"

"Cecil Train."

"Huh." Then his eyes were dead ahead again; he dropped the shift into drive.

"Hey. That's seven bucks."

"Oh, yeah," said the driver, drawing out the words. "You just put it on our tab, you hear? Cause we gonna be back. Yeah, we gonna be back." Then he gunned the motor; the Pontiac fishtailed slightly and sped down the dusty, empty street.

The young man in new overalls walked into Train's tiny store, which was empty at this hour and would be empty until after lunch, the stacks of canned goods and home conveniences and the displays of candy and ammunition and fishing tackle gathering dust silently in the weak winter light; he walked quickly down the store's center aisle, through the overheated cubicle where old Leo Train lay, asleep on a dusty cot, through the airless, impossibly cluttered back storeroom and into the bathroom. A single lightbulb hung from a dusty cord like an executed horsethief; the young man stared at his bloodless face in the grimy mirror over the sink, he wiped the cold sweat from his forehead and then vomited almost silently into the toilet. When he looked at his face again it was even whiter, and his eyes were full of tears; but he felt much better. He threw cold water on his face and the back of his neck; he dried his eyes with a sleeve and, smiling faintly, ran his fingers through his crew-cut hair.

When he walked back out front Leo was up, boiling water for instant coffee on the hotplate. The old man's white hair stood out all over his head, and silver whiskers glinted on his pointed chin; there was a rime of dried spittle at the corners of his mouth. The water began to bubble; with a trembling, age-spotted hand he poured it on the coffee, added a dollop of condensed milk and slowly, carefully, raised steaming cup to eager puckered lips. There was a quick tentative sip, then a longer one, then a barely controlled slurping; soon the cup was lowered, and Leo sighed with relief.

The young man positioned himself behind the counter, with an elbow propped against the cash register. He stared outside at Yarbee's deserted main street. He saw dust bits floating in a shaft of light; the word TRAIN'S, in chipped gilt letters, showed backwards on the streaked and dusty front window. Leo shuffled up to the counter in his fluffy blue slippers. An edge of yellowed cotton showed through his unbuttoned fly and his galluses hung in long loops at the sides of his legs. With one hand gripping the other at the wrist he carefully set a cup of coffee on the counter in front of the young man.

"Drink up," he said. "I'm gonna make me some toast.

You want some toast?" Then he was walking away, his head nodding like a pigeon's, before the young man could say yes or no.

The front door opened suddenly, making the tiny bell on a string jingle wildly. It was the county sheriff, a fat man dressed in khaki and a stiff wide-brimmed western hat. He was wearing two revolvers on his hips, pearl-handled guns in handsome holsters of tooled brown leather.

"Luckies," he said.

"Fifty cents."

The sheriff pounded one end of the pack against the counter, then with pudgy but surprisingly dainty fingers peeled away the cellophane and extracted and lit a cigarette. He leaned casually against the counter.

"Where's the old man?"

"In back."

"Who are you, boy?"

The young man stared blankly at the sheriff. "Buck," he said finally.

"Huh. Where'd Cecil go?"

"I don't know. I just started to work."

Leo lifted the edge of the curtain that separated his bedroom from the store and peered out. "Who's that? Is that the law?"

"That's right," said the sheriff loudly. He smiled at the young man and winked broadly. "I'm on a case, Leo." His deep voice fairly boomed in the empty store. "It's a sex case, Leo. We got five good women down in Madison that got raped real savage last night. And they say you're the one that did it." The sheriff leaned across the counter and poked an elbow at the young man; he winked again.

"What!" Leo burst dramatically through the curtain and shuffled quickly toward the counter in his fluffy slippers. "Now what's this?" He looked concerned; his brow was all wrinkled up and his eyes were narrowed. The sheriff was laughing softly; he winked again and again at the young man and placed a fat hand on Leo's white head.

"Them women say you're just a terror in the dark. One of them said if you wasn't such a beast, she would of even liked it."

"You go on."

"Yessir. A regular terror in the dark." The sheriff chuckled and winked; suddenly his smile was gone completely. "Hey. What happened to Cecil?"

"He's gone off to Alturas."

"What for?"

"To work on a ranch."

"No shit." The sheriff dropped his cigarette on the floor and stamped it out. "No shit," he said. "Don't know what he'd want to go up there for. It gets too cold in the mountains."

"They pay a good wage."

"I bet," said the sheriff. He looked down at the old man. "A heap better than his granddaddy pays, huh, Leo?"

"You go on, Sheriff." He pushed the fat man playfully in the stomach. "Go on, now. Get out of here." The sheriff let Leo push him toward the door. He exited, laughing, his huge bulk barely fitting between the jambs; the little bell rang daintily as he went. When he was gone Leo spat drily on the worn wooden floor of his shop.

By midafternoon there were five men clustered about

the portable electric heater that buzzed and glowed in the back of the store. The sheriff was there, with a fresh chili sauce stain on his shirt; his squad car was parked out front by the gas pump. He kept dozing off, sprawled in a wooden chair, his khaki-clad fat sagging sadly. The other men were silent for the most part. They sat in a rough half-circle around the heater, smoking; sometimes a throat would be cleared wetly or a chair would scrape against the wooden floor. Except for the sheriff, they were all old, bald and curiously shrunken. When they stood up their shiny heads barely showed over the shelves of canned food. They would walk slowly to the bathroom; in a minute the toilet would flush and the store would fill with the sounds of crashing waves and cascading waterfalls.

The young man, Buck, waited on the women who came in to buy groceries. They were gray-haired women with heavy, mottled faces; by some law of compensation they had put on the weight the old men had shed. They wore glasses in pastel-colored plastic frames, and their hair was stiffly "done" in silver-dollar curls. A Mrs. Seaman introduced herself and asked after Cecil.

"He's gone to work on a ranch in the mountains."

"Really? My goodness, I'm sure that's hard work. And who are you? Are you a Train?"

"No ma'am. I just happened along."

"Really? Well now. Are you from the county?"

"No."

"From Yono?"

"No."

She looked at him closely. Her eyes were hard to make out behind thick smudged glasses. "My goodness," she said.

Two younger women came in with a little girl of five or six suspended by her arms between them. She was Pearl Hartman; her golden hair was tied in two pony-tails and she was wearing her favorite school dress, a red dress with a pattern of tiny cows and pigs leaping over fences and barns. Nancy Hartman let her daughter drag her around the store; she kept leaning backwards like someone walking an energetic dog. Buck watched her graceful, backward-leaning head and neck glide up and down the aisles. She had dark hair hanging down her back and bangs across her forehead; she was saying "No, Pearl" every few seconds in a calm voice. The other woman stayed up front, looking at magazines. When nothing interested her she stared frankly at the old men around the heater. Once she caught the young man's eye and stared at him, without smiling, without any expression, until he looked away.

She walked up to him at the counter. "Where's Cecil?"

"He's gone to work on a ranch."

"A ranch? Whereabouts?"

"I don't know. You could ask Leo."

The woman looked puzzled for a moment, then mildly distressed. She stared over Buck's shoulder; she opened her purse and counted out change.

"Let me have a pack of Salems." She had a narrow fragile face; her skin was unusually pale, almost opaque where it was stretched across her forehead. There were wrinkles and shadows and circles like punctuation around her eyes, and her hair was yellow and silky like the little girl's.

"I'm Eva Gray," she said. She paused, watching him closely. "Did you know Cecil before he left?"

"No." She was staring at him; suddenly she smiled.

"Well." She put the Salems in her purse.

"Did you want to talk to Leo?"

"No."

Pearl and her mother were approaching the counter with their arms full of groceries. Pearl dropped a box of animal crackers on the floor, and when she stooped to pick it up she lost a bag of corn chips which she then stepped on, popping the plastic. Nancy Hartman cleaned up the spilled chips, apologized to the young man and fetched a new bag. Pearl gave him a guilty smile.

Eva looked down at the little girl. "Pearl, say you're sorry." Pearl looked blankly up at her and said nothing.

"Cecil's gone," Eva said to Nancy Hartman.

"Oh?" She dumped her groceries on the counter. They were facing each other, the two women; in profile they looked nearly identical with their sharp features and long necks. Eva was taller and older-looking, because of her pale skin and her bruised-looking eyes, edged with clusters of wrinkles like tiny river deltas. Her eyes looked tired, strained; she looked at things a little too long, at faces especially, as if insisting on her right to stare.

She slid a finger under the blonde hair at the back of her neck and flipped it up, tossing her head at the same time with a slow, luxurious motion. She stared at her sister, who was looking back calmly; time stopped temporarily, the young man's mouth dropped open and his breathing stopped; a second prolonged itself and he was struck permanently by the figure they made, a beautiful face gazing into its twin. Then the doorbell jingled; Pearl was going outside. His mouth was wide open like an idiot's and a string of drool was pulling down from the lip. Nancy and Eva looked away politely; he rang up the groceries and quickly put them in a bag.

II

When the store closed at six he went with Leo to eat dinner. They walked down Yarbee's darkening main street to the Elbow Room Cafe. It was brightly lit, warm and full of farm families dining out. Leo recommended a fried chicken dinner that came with soup, salad, fries and pie.

Leo ate very slowly. He chewed each bite carefully, methodically, his lips pursed tightly; he was afraid his dentures might come loose and clatter onto his plate. He sat perfectly erect and lifted each piece of food very slowly to his nervous mouth; sometimes a forkful would stall in mid-air, a broken elevator in an old hotel; he would look at Buck and open his mouth to speak, then close it, then open it and fill it with food.

"Now, Buck," he said once, a bite of pie trembling beneath his chin, "have you got a room somewheres?"

"No. I was thinking I'd sleep in the car."

He shook his head. "That's no way to live." He fit a bite of pie in his mouth and chewed and shook his head again. Soon he got up and walked to the back of the cafe. Buck watched him making a phone call; he came back smiling, with a bunch of toothpicks in his hand. "I happen to know of where there's a room for rent, a nice room in a nice house. It's Ed Gray's house. It's about six mile outside of town. Now I just called up, and Eva said it's a deal if you can pay ten bucks a week, but I wouldn't give her more than eight; that's what Cecil paid. Cecil liked it there, it's quiet and there's good food, and they don't bother you none. Ed Gray is a bit of a hardnose but he ain't around except a few days every two weeks. He drives for Navaho Truck, mostly down south. So what do you say?"

"All right."

Leo smiled and handed him a toothpick.

Buck drove out alone after supper in his old Chevy station wagon. It was a dark night, stars and moon blocked out by the ceiling of clouds. He flicked on his brights but there was nothing to see; the road stretched straight ahead, flat as any road he had ever been on. The fields on either side of the road were just as flat, silent and endless and unmarked. Sometimes he passed farmhouses, meagerly lit up in the dark and looking out of place and forlorn. He switched on the car heater and the radio. There was a single station coming in faintly through the roar of static; the music was quick and gay and the announcer spoke in Spanish.

He passed the litter can Leo had told him to watch for and the grove of young oaks, planted in neat rows. The driveway suddenly appeared and he turned onto it, his headlights swinging in a wide arc that briefly illumined the empty fields. The house sat back from the highway, a hundred yards or more along the straight unpaved drive. It was a two-story wood frame house with an unscreened porch. There was a black oak as tall as the roof in the front yard, its branches outlined by the bright porch light. He parked the Chevy and walked to the front door, which was covered with hundreds of insects, mosquitoes and black beetles and bees and moths, huge moths with intricate markings on their powdery wings.

Eva let him in. She was wearing a pink housecoat which she held closed at the neck. Her hair was rolled loosely in a bun. Ed Gray was sitting in an overstuffed chair with a newspaper covering his lap. He looked once at Buck and then away. The room glowed oddly in the flickering blue light of the TV.

Eva stared at him. She held the heavy front door open but said nothing; her face was expressionless; she stared. Something happened on the TV and her face was lit up. The blue light made her skin look deathly cold. Behind her the man in the chair lifted a beer can to his lips, took a quick sip, returned the can soundlessly to the polished surface of a table.

Buck fought an impulse to leave. There was something wrong about the room, something cold and distorted; it struck him as the kind of room where grisly crimes were committed. There was a dark rug on the floor and pale drapes on the windows, another overstuffed chair and bookshelves lined with paperbacks. An open door led off into darkness, presumably the kitchen.

"I forgot your name," Eva said.

"Buck." He walked in.

"That's Ed," she said, indicating him with a nod of her head. He was a large man, in his thirties, his muscle beginning to turn to fat; his hair was thin on top. There was an elaborate tattoo on his forearm, a fanged and fork-tongued viper curling around a flaming sword. He finished the can of beer with a long swallow and disappeared into the kitchen. He had a pronounced limp.

Eva led Buck across the living room and up the narrow staircase to the second floor. The house had a musty smell but it was neat, with many small framed pictures on the walls. The upstairs was chilly and sparely furnished; his room had a high bed and a chest of drawers, a full-length mirror and a curtained window. On one wall was a print of a three-masted schooner, and across the room was a watercolor on yellowed paper of an ocean sunset. Buck caught his reflection in the mirror; a warp in the glass made his head stand slightly to the side of his neck. He sat heavily on the bed and the springs creaked in alarm.

"Well?" She indicated the room with a sweep of her arm.

"It's fine. I'll take it."

She lifted up an edge of the curtain and stared out the window at the blackness. The hand which she had held at her neck fell to her side and the robe opened slightly, baring a long V of very white skin. The glass of the window reflected her darkly.

"Cecil Train was living here," she said. "Those are his jacket and such in the closet." She looked down at him, sitting on the bed; her gaze returned to the window. "Cecil was nice. Everybody liked Cecil. I guess I shouldn't say 'was,' I mean he still *is* nice, wherever he is; it's just that he won't be back, probably ever. Young people don't stay around here long, if they've got something going for them, because there's just nothing to do. You'll see after a while; it gets right tiresome." She came away from the window and stood in the middle of the room. The ceiling sloped down behind her, and from where Buck was sitting on the bed she looked unusually tall and thin, with her lank yellow hair and her narrow arms hanging out of the wide sleeves of the housecoat. Buck could see the pale edge of her breast where the neck of her coat fell open. She stared at him.

"Now tell me," she said. "What are you doing around here?"

He shrugged his shoulders. "Nothing."

"How come you're working down at Leo's?"

"Well, I just happened to come along. I went in there a few days ago to get a candy bar and Leo says, you want a job? So I thought, why not?"

"What were you doing in Yarbee?"

"Just traveling through."

"On your way to where?"

"Hey, what is this? Are you a cop or something?"

She laughed and tossed her head. "I'm just curious about my boarders, is all." She smiled at him; she waited a second and then sat down on the bed a couple of feet away from him, with her hands on her knees. He noticed a mole like a small raisin on her white neck. She smelled freshly of soap.

"Are you from California?"

"Yes."

"Where? The city?"

"Sort of."

"What do you mean, 'sort of'?"

"I used to live in the city. Then all around."

"But not around here."

"No." She gave him a look of exaggerated suspicion. Then she looked off into space; she bit at a fingernail; she seemed to have forgotten him.

"I know why you're here," she said suddenly.

"Why?"

"You're in hiding."

"No." She was staring at him skeptically. "No," he said again. He tried to look as if he meant it.

"Well then. You must like farmers."

"Sure."

"Or I know. You're an artist who's looking for the real thing."

"That's it."

She smiled at him. "Well, you picked the wrong county. This one is made up." When she smiled she was remarkably attractive; the wrinkles around her eyes became crinkles of good humor. She lifted both her arms to tuck some loose hairs into her bun, and Buck saw her full pale breast, the nipple and the under-curve pressed against the fabric of her housecoat.

A door slammed somewhere. Ed Gray came slowly up, his limp making an odd rhythm against the stairs. He passed Buck's open door without looking in. Eva smiled once again. "Wooden leg," she said. She got up slowly and followed him off to bed.

III

Buck woke up to the sounds of doors slamming, people talking loudly and something heavy crashing to the floor. His bedroom window faced east and the gray light which was coming in made the room look larger and dingier than it had the night before. It was cold in the room. He stayed in bed, caught in the warmth of the covers.

The full-length mirror faced the bed from across the room. He watched himself, a long mound of blankets ending in a shaven head with staring eyes. He threw off the blankets suddenly and marched across the cold floor to the mirror. His face was wide and bare as a melon. He looked like someone else, anyone else; his head was a volleyball made of skin. The warp in the mirror made it hard to focus. He felt weak in the knees and off balance; he turned away quickly and jumped back into bed.

When he came downstairs he found Ed Gray in the same chair watching a football game on the TV. He was drinking a beer and smoking; one leg was propped up on a hassock. Eva was in the kitchen, sitting at a table with her sister and a man Buck hadn't seen before. He was a short man on the thin side, maybe thirty-five or a little older. He was wearing denims, and he sat perfectly upright in his chair, his feet flat on the floor and his hands clasped loosely in his lap.

"Buck," said Eva. "Meet Herbie Hartman. And this is Nancy Hartman. My little sister." Herbie stood up and shook hands; he had an appealing face, a benign smile. He stood with his head slightly back, so that despite his height he seemed to be looking down at you, sighting along his thin nose. He pumped Buck's arm energetically.

There was a crashing sound nearby and Pearl emerged from the cellar, wearing a miniature suit of denims and with her yellow hair hanging loose. She stood behind her mother's chair and suddenly threw her arms around her neck, squeezing till the woman's face turned red and her eyes bugged. Then she let go and ran out of the kitchen, colliding briefly with Buck and slapping her father on the belly as she passed by.

"Buck is working down at Train's," Eva said.

"Well now," said Herbie Hartman. He was nodding his head and smiling. "Leo Train is OK. He's a good man. A little careful with his cash, but he's all right. Wouldn't you say, Buck?"

"I don't know."

"Well." Herbie sat back down at the table. He resumed his position, back straight, feet planted and hands clasped. "Leo is kin of mine. Let's see, he was an uncle to my father, or maybe it was a cousin. There was some dispute or other when my father died; Leo got left out and he was right mad. See, he claimed he was owed money from way back, when my father first bought land here by borrowing off of everyone he knew. According to Leo, if it weren't for him my old man would of never got off the ground. Would of starved. He was mad when he found out he wasn't left a cent. So I went down to see him, and he says, 'It ain't the land or the money, you understand; it's the insult.' That was all he'd say, 'It's the insult.' So I gave him a good piece of what I got out of it."

"Herbie, what are you telling that story for? The boy ain't interested in that."

"Now, how do you know, Nancy? And it ain't a story; it's the truth. Let the boy speak for himself. He'll tell me when he's heard enough."

"Sure I'm interested," said Buck.

"See? Well." Herbie Hartman smiled at his wife and Eva; then he smiled at Buck. "Leo's had that little store since before the war; let's see, 1940 or so, I'd guess. I used to go in there and steal gum and such off him. He never much cared. He did all right with that store from the beginning. It used to be if you wanted certain goods you had to go to Leo, because he had the only outlet in the county. It was a busy shop all the time; everyone in the county come in there some time or other every day, to get this or that. Now it's different, you see; there's much bigger stores in Stern, in the south of the county. But Leo's still doing all right, I imagine. What would you say, Buck, is he doing all right?"

"Sure."

"Well." Herbie looked pleased; now that his story was finished an expression of benign calm lit his face.

Ed Gray came into the kitchen. He crushed a beer can and threw it in the garbage, then opened the refrigerator and took out a fresh Coors. He returned to the front room; no one looked at him as he left.

After breakfast Buck drove the six dull miles into town. The sky was clouded over again, a gray and threatening ceiling to the endless dun-colored boredom of the flat fields. Now Buck saw the few farmhouses in detail. Most of them had a dusty oak or two in the front yard and a rusted wrecked car somewhere on the premises. There were chicken coops and privies behind the houses, and empty barns built of weathered wood. None of the houses had yards; at some the ground had been plowed right up to the front step. The doors were locked and the windows shuttered like sleeping eyes; there was no one in the fields and no one on the road.

He parked his car next to a phone booth a block before Train's store. He got out and looked around; the street was empty, there were no faces at the windows across the way. He stepped into the booth and had an operator make his connection to San Francisco. The phone rang a dozen times.

"Hello?"

"Mario. This is Buck."

"Who?"

"Buck."

"Listen, man, I don't know who you are or what you want, but get off my back."

"Hey, this is *me*, this is really me." He waited a moment; Mario said nothing. "Really. I'm calling from out of town."

"Is that really you?"

Buck laughed. "Sure. What's the matter, don't I sound right?"

"Yeah. You sound fine. Shit, man, we thought you were dead."

"No."

"We really thought you were dead. Those guys are rough, you know. First they was calling here every hour. Then they got hold of Ann one night when she was coming up the street and they beat on her till she told them which way you went. Then we didn't hear nothing for a few days, so we figured maybe they had got you. You better watch out, man, they're rough."

"I've seen them."

"Oh?"

"But they didn't recognize me. I've changed my looks."

"Jesus." There was a pause while they thought of what to say. Buck could hear the hum of the long-distance wires and, very faintly, two voices in conversation on the same cable.

"Where are you?"

"I don't know. A farm county somewhere."

"What's it like?"

"It's all right. I got a job and a room."

"Hey, what did you do with it?"

"Nothing yet."

"What are you going to do? I mean, what *can* you do with it up there?"

"I don't know. I'll just sit on it for a while." Buck heard Mario sigh. It was a long, theatrical sigh, a characteristic Mario sound.

"Hey, Mario," he said, "I miss you. I miss everybody."

"Sure."

"I wish I was back."

"Sure."

"I don't know what I did it for. I just got an urge, you know; I thought, why not? I just did it for the hell of it."

"Sure, I understand."

"It was just sitting there, begging to be taken. Anyway, I was tired of their bullshit. They act too tough."

"They *are* tough."

"No. They think they are. Look what I did to them, one punk with a quick hand."

"Yeah. But now they going to fix you."

"No they won't. They've got to find me first. I was right under their noses and they blew it."

"You was lucky."

"That's right. I'm lucky. And I'm smart, too. They're just stupid crooks with their head up their ass. I'm not worried about them."

"You better worry."

"What for? They're just stupid crooks. I'm not worried. Only thing I'm worried about is, how am I going to get rid of it? If I came back to the city they'd find me for sure. Hey, listen, maybe they'd want to buy it back."

"Are you kidding?"

"No. Why not?"

"Cause they don't operate like that. You fucked with them; they going to teach you a lesson."

"Come on."

"I'm serious. You should see what they done to Ann."

"Well. Then maybe I could just give it to them. That's what I could do. We could make a deal, they take off the heat, I give it back."

"No."

"Why?"

"Cause it's like I told you; you fucked with them. You can't just play around with guys like that."

"Well, shit. I just did it for the hell of it." It seemed so simple, he had acted on an impulse; it had almost been a joke. There had to be a way to undo it. There had to be a solution. He would think about it carefully; he was sure he would come up with something. "Well, OK," he said. "Just called to say I'm still alive. Say hello to everyone."

"All right."

"And tell Ann I'm awful sorry it happened."

"Sure."

"Tell her I might sneak down after a while, just to say hello. I could come down at night sometime and come in a window or something. Yeah, I think I might do that."

"Are you crazy?"

"Why, what's the matter?"

"I'll tell you what's the matter. If they see you around here they going to shoot you down. Dead. They got men sit in their car all day and all night, just praying for a chance at you. For them you are a dead man already. You understand? Already dead."

He was beginning to understand. "All right," he said. "Well. Take care of yourself."

"All right." He hung up the phone. He stood for a moment with his hand on the receiver, then walked down the block to Leo's.

IV

November passed; December and January and February passed, looking very much alike. He worked for Leo Train five and sometimes six days a week, selling cookies and corn chips and gas. The old women in their crusty hairdos came and went, and the old men stayed, sitting silently beside the electric heater at the back of the store. In January one of them died at five in the afternoon, just as Buck was walking by to fetch a case of Drāno. The man was John Weld, retired farmer, and he died without a word, sitting up with his hands on his knees. Buck saw the startled look frozen on his face; he tried to wake him up, and when that didn't work he got Leo and they carried him out of the store and drove him to the hospital in Stern, where he was pronounced dead. The rest of the men kept their seats. The next morning they all went to his funeral but by midafternoon they were back in the store, coughing and talking occasionally and waiting by the side of the heater.

The sky was always gray. Herbie Hartman, who came in to the store two or three times a week and who spent considerable time leaning against the front counter talking to Buck and to anyone else who wanted to listen, explained that the weather in Royo County was like that; in the winter, which began in November and lasted till April, the sky was always gray and the air was always chilled and dry, except for the rare times when, with great relief, it rained. Then in the summer, which began in April and lasted through October, the sky was perfectly cloudless and blue, sharp deep blue, so blue you sometimes begged for a cloud or a haze, for anything that would interrupt that blue perfection. But the only thing you ever got were a few clouds at the end of the day, fleecy strings of cloud that came from nowhere and meant nothing as far as the weather was concerned. They were strictly ornamental, according to Herbie; they enlivened the lingering Royo sunsets, and then disappeared as the first stars came out.

Herbie knew everything about the county. He knew the oddities of the weather and the land; he knew what you ought to farm and what you ought not, and where you could market and what you could expect there. He was the son of a local farmer, as he explained, and before that he was the grandson and the great-grandson of people who had farmed up north, and before that he was descended from people who had farmed somewhere in Europe, England or Germany, he wasn't sure which. He knew everyone in the county, no exceptions made, and every person was a story. Old people were worth dozens of stories; even the local kids could spark him to tales of where and how they were born, and how their parents had gone about mating, and how they were likely to turn out, given the oddities of their lineage. Herbie would stand in the front of Leo's store, his hip pressed against the check-out counter and his ankles casually crossed, his head tilted back as he held forth on whatever pricked his interest. The stout Royo women in permanents and bifocals would sneak past him, sliding their purchases under his gesturing arms; then they would stand to one side, politely silent, with a hawk's eye for Buck as he rang up the bill.

He liked to listen to Herbie talk. He relaxed and let the stories flow on; nothing was expected of him in the way of a response, Herbie made that clear, so he could tune in or out whenever he wanted without giving offense. It was a perfect form of entertainment; the stories were simple and relaxed, they went on and on at an easy pace till they ran into a point, or till they spawned other stories, and those stories other stories, like a jungle growing relentlessly before your eyes. It hardly occurred to him to believe or disbelieve Herbie's stories; actually they were all a bit too fantastic to believe. They were about the local people, it was true, but about their oddest features—their scars and warts and fatal ailments, or their love affairs and feuds. In Herbie's stories everyone was bizarre; everyone had an odd lump somewhere on his figure, or a disgraceful episode tucked away in an airless closet. Take John Train, the big bald handsome man who came in a couple of times every week. He was Leo's oldest son, and everything about him was easy—his soft lisping voice, his shy smile, his gentle manner. But he was a killer, according to Herbie; he had been seven years in Soledad prison for the hatchet murder of his wife's young Mexican lover. And then there was Mrs. Ben Seaman, from Yono County, who came in often and exchanged pleasantries with Buck and Leo. She was a woman of fifty with a haggard face and legs like huge salamis in her brown ski pants; Herbie let it be known she had been born without nipples or a sexual orifice, and that these had been constructed surgically when she was still a baby.

"Oh, come on," Buck said.

"I swear to God."

"No nipples—how do you know about that?"

"I heard tell. Her daddy and my daddy were like that," he said, curling two fingers together. "You know how it is; things get said, over the years."

Did Buck want to know how Ed Gray lost his leg? Well, it had happened just a few years back, in a freak accident. You see, Ed loved fresh trout, or any type of fresh fish, but he didn't much care for fishing, which was boring. So he and Noodles Pisco—who was the sheriff now that Martin Zinger was gone and because no one else in the entire county wanted the job and because Noodles was in the habit of looking elsewhere when people got into mischief, unless of course they happened to be Mexicans—well, Ed Gray and Noodles had heard there was more than one way to get a freezer full of fresh-caught trout. So they had gone up to a river somewhere in Humboldt County with a few sticks of dynamite, and whenever they had seen a likely looking hole they had tossed in a charge that would go off underwater and send up dozens of dead fish, a little shredded but good eating just the same. Except that Ed had slipped on a muddy bank once, and followed the dynamite into the water; there had been an explosion, and Noodles had pulled him out of the stream unconscious, with his leg below the knee ripped off like a chunk of wood. It had looked really terrible, Noodles said. Well, Ed had never been what you would call an easy-going fellow, and the accident turned his mind completely for a while; he calmed down after a month or two, but he was mean afterwards, and sour, and silent. Eva couldn't stand him anymore; sometimes he scared her half to death, she said. But she went to work and made enough to pay for the hospital and a false leg carved out of some new lifelike plastic. It was an amazing gadget; he couldn't walk too good on it but it was fine for driving a truck. Ed had got that truck job way back in the fifties, after he won his trial; let's see, what had the charges been? Something crazy; a morals charge, something like that. Did Buck want to know about Ed Gray's trial?

No, he didn't really believe Herbie's stories; they were too fantastic. People weren't that bizarre, especially these people, farmers and the wives and children of farmers, born and grown up and destined to die in this flattest, driest, most uniform and boring landscape he had ever seen. They came into the store day after day in the same clothes, with the same greetings on their lips, in need of yet another tin of Crisco; they stood in front of the cash register blank-faced, silent, unaware, cattle before the ax; they paid and exited to the chilly street and then disappeared completely. He couldn't keep all their names straight, they looked and acted so alike. With few exceptions the women were middle-aged and overweight; except for the few in the rear of the store the men were all big and silent, with rough hands and meat-slab faces. There were a few young children, shy and dumb-looking and fond of punching each other, but almost everyone older than fifteen and younger than fifty was gone, presumably to the city. He felt like a man from another race, disguised in his short hair and overalls and sent to spy on the country creatures; he would study their curious habits and learn the secret behind their dull faces.

Except that there wasn't any secret, of course; the dull faces weren't sly masks, they were windows on more dullness. He really didn't know what kept him around. Several times he had gotten set to leave but had decided against it at the last moment. He wasn't safe there, the black men in the Pontiac would be back, he was sure of it; still he felt safe, for no good reason. Maybe it was the boredom itself, the flat land and the dull faces that made him think nothing outrageous or explosive could ever happen there. Anyway, he had stayed; he thought he would leave in a little while.

V

He was feeling dull himself after so many months in Royo County, with nothing to do but work and listen to Herbie Hartman and eat greasy chicken with Leo at the Elbow Room, and then go home to the Grays' and maybe talk to Eva some. He liked her, she had a way; they talked a lot. She looked sickly, thin and pale, especially now that it was winter. She didn't do much but keep the house and read paperbacks, mostly science fiction and Luke Short western adventures. In the evenings he would come home from Yarbee and find the whole house dark except for the glaring light over the kitchen table where Eva was sitting, still in her quilted housecoat, surrounded by paperbacks and Salem butts. She would glance up as he came in, smile briefly, then go back to her book; she was afraid of looking eager for his company, so it was he who had to start the conversations. Then when he had sat down she would erupt into words, talking nonstop and with obvious relief for a few minutes, till the sharpest edge of her need was gone.

Ed was away most of the time. He would come back late at night and go immediately to the tube; when he left three or four days later there would be pounds of crushed beer cans in the garbage. Eva slept with him but rarely spoke to him, and never spoke of him when he was gone. They seemed to coexist; there was something hard and ill between them; they were waiting for something to happen.

When Ed was back Eva was a tight wire, rigid with control. Nancy Hartman usually came to visit then. She looked good, a handsome, erect woman with fine long hands and color in her cheeks. She was quiet and warm; Eva relaxed in her presence. She often brought Pearl along and let her storm through the house. The little girl spent hours in the basement doing nothing but running and colliding with things. Sometimes Buck went down to keep her company. The basement was cold and wet, the source of the mustiness that pervaded the house, but Pearl didn't seem to mind. She would capture furry spiders and the giant black beetles that gushed a yellow cream when you stepped on them, and she would walk up to Buck and gently lay them in his hand, as if they were fragile treasures. Then she would run off and throw herself headlong onto a pile of rags, or start pounding empty oil cans with a stick, or pull garden tools and empty cartons off the shelves that lined the walls.

She was a beautiful child with pale yellow hair, like

Eva's, and a simple, unexpressive face. There was nothing complicated or sly about her face; it was perfect, like a pearl, oval and smooth and self-evident. She wore the same alert and serene expression no matter what she was doing, sitting in her mother's lap with thin arms around her neck, or gathering spiders in the basement's musty crevices. She rocked the house with her energy. She attacked everyone, indiscriminately; she liked to collide with people, to punch as well as caress. Even Ed Gray attracted her attentions; she was fond of sneaking up behind his chair and leaping onto his lap, so that he lost his wind with a gasp and spilled beer down his shirt front. He seemed to like her attacks. He let her sit or kneel on his belly, and do her worst with her fists; she would work him over and then curl up against his chest and watch the football game for a while. One morning Buck surprised them in the middle of a tussle, Pearl using Ed for a trampoline and Ed laughing uncontrollably, like a kid; Pearl got up and left and as Buck passed by he saw the sweat on Ed's glowing face and the small tent she had made of his lap.

The many evenings Ed was gone Buck and Eva spent together. Buck would come home and talk to her in the kitchen and, if he was at all hungry, eat the pie or ice cream she served up. She told him about the books she was reading. The Luke Shorts were all the same, she didn't know why she read them; someone was always seeking vengeance, or some nakedly evil man had designs on a good woman's money; they were all the same and she knew how they would end, still it gave her pleasure when the crook was shot to death. She liked the science fiction even better; they were full of wild, dizzy ideas that stretched your mind out of shape, so that it took a few minutes when you were finished to know exactly where you were: in the yellow kitchen, in the musty dark house alone on the flat fields like a ghost ship at sea. She told him the plots of her favorite books in great detail; he liked to listen, he liked the way she talked. She talked rapidly, staring at him, gesturing with a cigarette that left crazy trails of smoke in the air. Or she would stand at the stove fixing cocoa, holding her robe closed with one hand and talking over her shoulder.

Sometimes they watched the late show together. She sat in Ed's chair with her legs tucked under her and made comments on the action. One night he brought home a pint of whiskey from Leo's and they watched an old movie and got drunk. Jennifer Jones was a peasant girl who talked to angels, and who was reviled by the townspeople until she led them to the miraculous spring at Lourdes. Eva hated Jennifer Jones; Jennifer's most pious acts made her grunt in disgust; when Jennifer died of cancer at the end of the movie, Eva beamed with satisfaction. The pint was soon gone; they were both pretty drunk. When Buck stood up he felt dizzy but amorous. He shut off the TV and the room was totally black. With his arms outstretched and his fingers groping, he walked over to Eva and pulled her to her feet.

"No," she said. He kissed her hard on the mouth. He pushed his tongue against her tightly sealed lips. She put a hand on his chest and pushed him away.

"Nope," she said. He couldn't see but he heard her hair swish as she shook her head. "Nope," she said.

Alone in his bed he thought about her and wanted

her. The dark room was spinning and wobbling, like a top that slowed down but refused to stop; still he wanted her, the desire mingling with a nausea that came in waves. Finally he decided: he would storm into her bedroom and throw himself on her, regardless of her protests. The more he thought about it the better an idea it seemed; it was what she herself wanted, he convinced himself; she wanted to be forced a little. She was probably disappointed in him now, lying alone in her double bed wondering what was keeping him away. He threw off the covers and staggered out of bed, but halfway across the room the top picked up speed till it was spinning fiercely on an irregular axis, till his body was jerking like a sleeper who dreams he is falling, and he detoured just in time to the bathroom. Afterwards he was only strong enough to get back in bed. He slept without dreams and woke with a dull headache.

He still came home and sat with her in the yellow kitchen and talked. She seemed pleased as well as relieved now when he came home. She talked about Nancy and Herbie Hartman, and about the rest of her family, all dead, and about Pearl, who the psychologist said was "emotionally disturbed" or "mentally defective," she forgot which; maybe he said she was both. She talked very little about Ed Gray; he had lost his leg in a hunting accident, she said. Buck listened. Sometimes he talked but for the most part he listened. He wanted her and he started thinking about her, especially when he was in bed. He thought of her in her quilted housecoat, with her hair put up in a sloppy bun; she always came to him, lying down softly in the bed without a word, then slowly peeling away the housecoat before pressing up against him with her eyes closed.

There was a large tiled bath between their bedrooms, and most mornings he woke up to the sound of her splashing and flushing. She liked to turn the shower up so hot that even the bedrooms filled with steam. He would stare at himself in the misted-over mirror across the room, and the day would start with a fantasy of Eva, skin pink and hot, suddenly striding out of the bathroom and into his stale bed. But she never did; the water would shut off with an echoing hiss; her wet feet would slap against the floor tiles; her towel would ring as it slid off the metal rack, and then the door to her bedroom would open and click shut.

One Saturday he came home and found her freshly bathed and wearing a flowered dress, stockings and high-heeled shoes. Her hair was brushed down her back.

"Let's go out," she said.

"OK."

"I know a place. A bar."

They drove down to Yarbee, to a bar called Zinger's Oasis on the main street across from the cafe. There were neon Budweiser signs winking in the small front windows, and inside the bar was pine-paneled, warm and full of people drinking beer. The floor was covered with sawdust and peanut shells. They stepped past two couples dancing in front of the jukebox and found an empty booth. Eva put her purse beside her on the seat, threw back her hair, clasped her hands on the edge of the table and smiled at Buck.

"Well," she said. "I'm ready to have a good time."

He went to the bar and got a pitcher of beer, which they drank slowly. The couples by the jukebox were dancing to a sad country song. A woman in a sequined skirt and white plastic boots was pressed hard against her man; she was dancing on tiptoe, with her face buried in her partner's neck. Buck watched as the man's hand snaked down her back and under the spangled edge of her skirt. The man was tall and bald, with a handsome gentle face; Buck suddenly remembered an ax, and seven years in Soledad, and the rest of the story Herbie had told about John Train.

"Hey, look at that." Eva was pointing across the room, to where Sheriff Noodles Pisco was sitting on a bench with his arms around two hard-looking women. Noodles was wearing his khaki uniform, including his wide-brim suede stetson. He was shaking with laughter; one of the women, a blonde in a low-cut blouse, was laughing with him, but the other woman looked bored. She was smoking fiercely and looking around the bar-room.

"Why, you know who that is?" Eva indicated the bored-looking woman. Then she shook her head.

"Who is it?"

"No one. I thought it was Lilian Pisco for a minute, Noodles' wife. She ran off last year with some other man. But that ain't her, I don't think. Now where did Noodles Pisco, fat as he is, get two good-looking women?"

"Maybe they like cops."

"Cops is one thing; Noodles is another." She took a long sip of beer, which left a foam mustache on her lip. She tapped out a Salem from a new pack and Buck lit it for her.

"Is this your regular bar?"

"No. Do I look like I hang out in bars?" She smiled reproachfully.

"It's a nice bar. Look, everyone's having a good time." He pointed at John Train, who was kissing his partner passionately while they stood in the middle of the dance floor. With his strong farmer's hands gripping her ample buttocks, he had lifted her several inches off the ground.

"He's crazy. That's Leo's son, did you know? He's really nuts. Ed got in a fight with him once and nearly got beat to death."

"What were they fighting about?"

"Nothing. Over me, I guess. That was years ago, when I was still young and attractive."

"You're still attractive."

"No I'm not."

"What do you mean? I'm telling you, you're attractive. You're very attractive." She looked skeptical. He took a sip of beer. "Really," he said. "I think you're beautiful."

"Oh, come on."

"No, I'm serious. You're the best-looking woman around. In the whole county."

"Well, that's not saying much. They're all grandmothers."

"All right, the best-looking in the state, then." She was laughing at him, with her eyes half-closed. She looked sleepy and warm, with her eyes half-closed and a line of foam drying on her lip. "Really," he said. "I love to look at you. I love to hear you talk." She stopped laughing; she licked her lip and swallowed.

He looked off at the dance floor. John Train and his girl were grinding and swaying against each other. The music stopped but they continued to dance. John was dressed all in black, from high-heeled black cowboy boots to black silk shirt; with his long groping arms he looked like a dancing tree. A man slipped a quarter into the jukebox and a new song came on; it was a fast number sung by a woman backed up by a fiddle and a whining steel guitar. John and the girl in white boots continued their undulating dance.

They drank their way through two pitchers of beer. Eva pointed out people in the crowd, people she had liked or known in one way or another. A stocky man with pointed sideburns came and stood at the end of their table. He had his hands on his hips, and he smiled down at Eva for a moment before saying anything. Buck noticed his gleaming silver belt buckle; it was a large rectangular buckle, with a tiny six-gun and rearing stallion attached to the metal.

"Hey, Eva," he said. "Where's your old man?"

"He's driving down to Tucson."

"Well now."

"Moon Cargo, this here is Buck." Moon nodded briefly in his direction. "What are you doing, standing there? You want a seat?"

"No, no."

"Well, what do you want?"

"You know me, Eva, I like to dance."

She shook her head.

"Come on, just one dance."

"I don't think so." She looked at Buck.

"Go on," he said.

"No."

"Go on."

"Well. All right." She stood up carefully and smoothed

down her dress. Moon put an arm around her waist and danced off with her. She looked stiff and cross in his tight embrace.

Buck left the table and located the men's room. He found Noodles Pisco at the urinal, legs spread wide and massive body leaning backwards as he fumbled with his fly. There was silence for several seconds; Noodles cleared his throat roughly, a cold engine trying to start; then came the hiss of piss against porcelain.

Noodles looked over his shoulder and under the brim of his stetson.

"Who's that?" he said.

"It's Buck."

"Who?" He looked again. "Oh. Leo's boy." He ducked his head and concentrated on business for half a minute. When he turned around his pecker was still between his two fingers; he flicked it once, twice, then tucked it away. "You see that pussy out there, boy?"

"Who?"

"Not who; *what*. I say, did you see that pussy I'm with?"

"Yes."

"That's some fine pussy, ain't it?"

"Sure."

"You bet it is." Noodles moved to the sink and with dainty efficient motions washed his neat pink hands. "Yessir," he said, "that's some mighty fine pussy. And it's all free, you understand. It's free pussy." He pressed a finger against Buck's chest; Buck caught the full force of the sheriff's beery breath. "You know what I mean— 'free pussy'?"

"No, what's that?"

"Huh." The sheriff smiled; he winked broadly. "Well,

that's what you get when you're sheriff. Yessir." He winked again; he gave Buck's chest a final poke. He edged sideways through the bathroom door.

When Buck got back to the booth he found Moon Cargo occupying his seat. Moon and Eva seemed to be arguing; they stopped when they saw him approach.

"Hi," she said. "Moon was just getting up."

"No I wasn't. I like it here."

Buck looked down at him. He tried to look threatening. "That's my seat," he said. His voice sounded weak; he was afraid it might crack.

"No it ain't, sonny." Moon was looking at Eva. He forced his fingers into a pocket of his skin-tight pants and pulled out a quarter. "Here," he said. "Go buy yourself a drink."

"I don't want a drink."

"Well, then just get lost."

"Moon Cargo, get out of here," Eva said. "You're a bigmouth and a bully. Go on, get out. I don't like the sight of you." Moon was staring at her and smiling; Buck watched the smile slowly fade.

"What did you say?"

"I said, get lost. You heard me right the first time. I don't want you hanging around."

Moon stared at her.

"You heard the lady," Buck said. His heart was thumping wildly, it was vibrating painfully right where Noodles had poked him in the chest.

Moon stood up. "All right, Eva," he said. "All right. But you're gonna regret this." He edged out of the booth.

"I don't regret nothing. You're just a bully, Moon Cargo. Besides, you're right ugly."

"You're gonna regret those very words," said Moon, nodding his head. Then he left, pushing his way roughly past Buck.

They stayed until the Oasis closed, at two. Walking to the car through the chill dark night, Eva rested her head on Buck's shoulder and put an arm around his back. They got in the Chevy and drove slowly down the county road. The lights were out in the few farmhouses; it was a cold night and Eva was pressed up against him, shivering slightly. He pulled into the driveway and stopped some fifty yards from the house. He kissed her; her mouth was warm and slack at first, tasting both sweet and sour from the beer and the Salems. She was very quiet and still. For a second he was afraid she had stopped breathing; he pulled back and saw that her face was perfectly calm, eyes closed and mouth faintly smiling.

He kissed her again, hard, and she opened up, pressing her body against him and grinding with her mouth, sliding her tongue in his mouth and sucking away his breath. He was almost afraid of her force; she slid her face from side to side, making his nose crack painfully. She pulled up her knees and he slid his hand down between her legs, feeling where the grainy stocking texture gave way to the buttery texture of thigh, and then, surprise, to the moist silky cushion of a crotch without panties. He ran his hand along the smooth small globes of her ass and into the warm sweaty crack between. He made a rake of his fingers and pulled it gently through her muff of hair. He slipped two fingers in her; her mouth was against his ear and she said "Oh" once, very distinctly, and then made a throaty sound, a growl; he thought for a split second of Noodles, clearing his throat while he waited at the pisser; then Eva was working her hips languorously against his fingers, and he was flooded with excitement, his cock hard and only seconds from coming in the prison of his blue jeans. She pulled away from him suddenly; she lifted her dress up around her waist and lay down, with one knee against the steering wheel and the other leg thrown over the back of the seat. Buck struggled with his belt and button fly; he forced his pants down to his ankles and pulled up his shirt, and then with great urgency and a groan of relief he climbed into her long open body. The front seat of the Chevy shook and squeaked for a minute and then was still.

They walked silently up to the dark house. Eva opened the front door and a gust of musty air hit their faces like a fleeing ghost. She disappeared inside. Buck waited at the threshold, expecting the lights to go on. But after a minute she reappeared, silently took his hand and led him through the pitch-black living room, up the hollow-sounding stairs and into his room.

"Why don't we use your bed?"

"I don't like it." She slipped out of her dress; he heard her stockings peel off in the darkness.

"Why not?"

"I just don't."

Buck undressed and climbed into the bed. Her body was warm and smooth under the cold sheets. He ran his hands all over her; she was smooth everywhere, her body was unusually long and smooth, boney just at the shoulders and in the space between her breasts. He kissed her breasts; they were long and fluid, they tended to disappear when she lay on her back. Her chest smelled faintly of sweat and talcum powder. He sucked at her nipples, holding them in his mouth and pulling back gently, so that they got hard quickly and then soft again, enlarged and sensitive. She stroked his back lightly with her fingernails. Her long arm reached down to his ass; her fingers settled between his legs and slithered there, like friendly snakes; then she took him in her hand and squeezed firmly. He said "Eva" suddenly, as if she had squeezed her own name out of him. She was breathing in his ear; he found himself breathing in the same rhythm, excited by her excitement; he rolled on top of her, eased his tongue in her mouth and slipped inside her. They made love slowly, carefully, keeping the lid on for a long while; he was wetly buried in her and she was split wide by his heavy rocking body; her legs locked him in place and her hands on his ass guided him around, a visitor to all her rooms. They fell asleep together and Buck woke up at the instant of sunrise, still on top of her. He rolled off carefully, organized the wreck of blankets and sheets and went back to sleep.

Ed was gone for another two weeks. They spent the nights in Buck's bed; they were long nights, full of sex and sweat. They would talk or watch the tube downstairs; around ten he would take a shower and get in bed; after a while Eva would turn out the living room lights and come silently up to his room. Every time she crawled in beside him Buck felt the same thing: he felt rich and full of possibilities; Eva lying next to him, long and eager, filled him up with expectations, none of them specific and all of them glowingly positive; he felt like they had all the time in the world. Thinking about her, lying in bed waiting for her to come up, gave him a hard-on; when she arrived their bodies would come together immediately, almost without it being willed. Then they would lie back, panting and heated up; after a while they would start to touch and then they were at it again, pounding away or else gliding smoothly together, like lazy fish, synchronized and relaxed.

Eva felt no guilt; she was amused. His body was white, young, and unused; at least it looked unused; he looked much younger without his clothes on. She felt sort of wicked, like a scheming older woman; it was a nice feeling. The whole thing was crazy and unreal; Ed would probably find out, and then what would happen? But she couldn't think about that, couldn't imagine it. Was this really happening? None of it seemed to count, somehow; that was part of why she liked it. She could just relax and enjoy herself, lay back and have her lover as much as she wanted.

She felt luxurious and sexy. She thought about him off and on during the day, while she was working around the house or sitting in the kitchen reading Luke Short. She pictured him in her mind; she thought about his voice, his large hands which were never in a hurry, his wide back and his muscular white ass. She started looking at herself in mirrors. She liked the way she looked, not quite so pale and her forehead no longer furrowed like a prune. She stared at herself in the mirrors; she had lovely eyes—they were still lovely— and at least she wasn't fat; she turned her head from side to side and admired the sharp planes of her face. There was a mirror in Buck's room that showed her full-length; it had a warp near the top, so she had to bend down to examine her face. One morning when they were making love she had looked over Buck's shoulder and seen their reflection across the room; they looked so busy, two bodies bouncing against each other, with all the detail of the immediate connection, wet penis in spread vagina, nakedly revealed; she had stared at them in the mirror, feeling detached and more excited.

VI

One unusually cold Wednesday, Herbie and Nancy Hartman came by the house. It was raining lightly, there was a cold mist on everything outdoors, and brief banks of fog were rolling on and off the county roads. The Hartmans were going to Redding for a few days, to do some business and to see Herbie's great-aunt Ida, who was suffering from a lung disease. She was a woman well over ninety, with a shrunken body and thick pure white hair; despite her age and her disease, her mind and memory were perfectly clear. Actually she had been suffering and threatening to die for as long as Herbie had known her. He didn't expect her to die soon, he explained; she talked too much about dying really to be ready for it; he just liked to see her and hear her nasty stories about all the long-dead Hartmans and Raineys.

They left Pearl at Eva's house. She had to stay so that she could see her psychologist in Stern and go to her special school, which met just three days a week. She seemed neither happy nor sad to see her parents go; she watched silently from the front door as Herbie and Nancy climbed in their old pickup and backed down the muddy drive. When they were out of sight she started to cry. Eva put her arms around her and immediately she cheered up. She stuck a cold tiny hand inside Eva's housecoat and pressed it to her warm skin; Eva let out a gasp and Pearl ran off laughing, crashing through the kitchen and down the cellar stairs.

Eva roamed through her house, looking for something to do. There was nothing to read, and the house was fairly clean. She hated to clean up; she hated to dust, to wash, to straighten, to scrub, mop, scour and shine. She had never gotten any appreciable satisfaction from performing those tasks; still, she did them, but reluctantly and not too well. It had never occurred to her to refuse. Her house was usually "in order," rather than "clean." It often happened that one of her rooms would look fine, even spotless from a certain distance, and yet there would hang over it a distressing dinginess, as if the windows had never been opened or someone had been sick there for a long time.

Sometimes rooms in her house gave off odd, vaguely unpleasant odors that lingered for days. They were odors without origins, the vague sour smells of an old country house. After you had been inside for a while they were hardly noticeable; Eva was used to ignoring them completely. But on this particular Wednesday she encountered an unusually sharp smell in the living room. It was more than a sharp smell: it was a terrible smell, and it seemed to be getting stronger and stronger the more she sniffed. The room was in good order, the chairs and the hassock and the TV were all in place; the floor was clear, the wastebasket empty, the bookshelves tidy though dusty. She stood in the middle of the room and sniffed. The smell seemed to grow in her nose; it was a cheesy, rotten smell, sour and powerful. She looked behind the drapes over the front window but found nothing. She stood on one of the chairs and peered over the top of the bookshelf; there was a lot of dust up there, a very old apple core and the skeleton of a mouse, but nothing that could cause that terrible smell.

She walked around the room in her housecoat, sniffing, trying to zero in on the source of the smell. She wasn't thinking about anything, just sniffing, and then suddenly she was thinking about her husband. The cheesy, yeasty smell grew stronger and she could see Ed's face before her, perfectly distinct. Her forehead furrowed up automatically; she clutched her housecoat tightly at the neck. She turned around suddenly, half-expecting to see him. But there was nothing there, only the terrible smell of something rotting.

She stood in the middle of the room and carefully sniffed in all directions. Ed would be back soon, dragging his phony leg behind him, and what would happen then? She would have to go to him and minister to his peculiar desires, and sleep with him in that sour, angry bed. And if he found out about Buck anything could happen; no, only one thing could happen, he would kill somebody. Eva turned a circle in the middle of the living room, her sniffing nose attached to the rotten odor; now it seemed to be coming from the TV side of the room, now from the direction of the chairs. She saw Ed, his large meaty face scowling and threatening like a huge fist. She knew him, he had been angry for a long time. He would kill somebody without even thinking. It would be a great relief for him to kill someone.

Eva gagged slightly on the smell. It really seemed to be getting stronger while she stood there, trying to sniff it out. She pinched her nose for a minute and breathed through her mouth. She kept thinking of Ed, his face was like a vision in front of her. She thought of when she had first seen him in the hospital, after the accident; he was sitting in bed, his bandaged stump on top of the blankets. His hands were clenched in bloodless white fists and he said nothing at all, he only stared at her, crazy with anger. He was so angry, so completely angry that she felt what had happened to his leg was somehow her fault. She had gone right to work to buy him a plastic leg. She hadn't even thought twice about it; it had never occurred to her to say no.

She could see his angry face staring at her. She knew he wasn't around but she was scared, just thinking of him. He was too angry; there was no arguing with someone who could be that angry. Eva unpinched her nose and took a tentative sniff. The smell was still there, potent as ever. The cellar door clattered open and Pearl came running into the living room. She stopped short in front of Eva and cocked her head to one side.

"What stinks?"

"I don't know. I can't find it."

Pearl started sniffing the air. She took a few steps toward the window, stopped, turned around, sniffed thoughtfully and began advancing on the overstuffed chairs. She sniffed the top of the hassock for a moment and shook her head. She pressed her face into the seat of Ed's chair and sniffed forcefully. She got on her hands and knees and smelled the upholstery. She smelled the little curtain of fabric that hung between the bottom of the chair and the floor. She stuck her head under the curtain and stayed there for several seconds.

She pulled her head out and looked blankly at Eva. "There," she said.

Eva got down on the floor and peered under the curtain. The smell was terrible and she was afraid of what she would find; it had to be something big and awful to smell so putrid. She reached tentatively under the chair and touched something furry. She jerked her hand back and gagged. She examined her hand; it looked all right, but what had she touched? She took a deep breath through her mouth, screwed up her face and reached under the chair again. She felt the furry surface, it was more fuzzy than furry, she got a hold on it and began pulling it out; her hand was shaking, she was ready to drop the thing and scream. Pearl looked on impassively as Eva's shaking hand brought the thing out from under the chair and into the light.

It was an old beer can, one that Ed had forgotten. It was covered all over with green mold. Eva looked at it sideways, her face averted, but Pearl put her nose right up to it and even touched the green mold, which hugged the can like a little fur coat.

"Ugh," said Eva. "What a stink." Pearl was poking a finger into the mold. She stuck her finger into the hole where the tab top had been and pulled out what looked like a black piece of string. She lifted it up; the partially disintegrated body of a small drowned rat emerged, covered with mold and dripping flat beer.

"Oh God," Eva said. She made Pearl drop the rat back in and she marched to the back door of the house, with the reeking parcel held at arm's length in front of her. She stepped outside into the light rain and hurled Ed's beer can as far as she could into the muddy fields. She spat after it; she snorted through her nose to clear it out. She stared out in the fields, shook her head, spat once again, then walked back in the kitchen and washed her hands.

She felt much better. She opened up all the downstairs windows to air out the house. Pearl was sitting in the kitchen, sniffing her fingers. Eva made her wash her hands. She felt thoroughly relieved. Ed's face was gone from her mind. She was tired of being scared, she decided. That was all he was to her, a bad scare; she didn't feel anything for him, not love certainly, nothing warm, not pity either. All that had been scared away. She sat down at the kitchen table, crossed her legs and lit a cigarette. She held the match and let it burn down; the flame grew smaller and smaller and went out just before reaching her fingers. I'm through, she said to herself. Then she said it out loud: "I'm through."

Pearl walked up to her, bounced her pelvis several times against Eva's crossed legs and grabbed her sleeve. "Animals," she said. Her face was blank.

"What are animals, honey?"

Pearl chewed the air. "Animals," she said.

"Oh," said Eva. "Well, I don't have any."

Pearl opened her mouth wide and stared sadly at Eva.

"How about an apple, honey? Or a banana?" She fetched a banana from the bunch that was sitting on top of the refrigerator. She peeled it and handed it to Pearl.

Pearl stuck an end of the banana in her mouth and sucked on it without chewing. After a few seconds she pulled it out and dropped it on the kitchen table. "Animals," she said.

"All right." Eva picked up the wet banana and dropped it in the garbage. "We'll have to go get you some animals."

VII

Buck was standing behind the counter, listening to Sheriff Noodles Pisco, who had been in the store all afternoon, teasing Leo Train and talking mysteriously about a trip he was about to make to Sacramento.

"Yessir," Noodles was saying, "it's part business and part pleasure. Know what I mean? First you take your pleasure, which involves a lot of business for this guy"— he winked suggestively and pumped his fist rapidly over the crotch of his tight khaki pants—"and then you do your business, which is just a pleasure. You got that straight, Leo?" Noodles laughed and winked at Buck. "Yessir," he said. He suddenly spread his legs and his arms wide, stuck his huge behind in the air and began advancing on Leo, his tongue hanging out and his pelvis jerking back and forth. Leo shuffled quickly towards the back of the store in his fluffy blue slippers. The sheriff threw back his head and laughed.

The bell on the front door sounded musically and in came Eva and Pearl. They were wearing yellow raincoats and clear plastic rainbonnets over their blonde hair; they looked like small and large versions of each other. Pearl suddenly tore away from Eva and disappeared down the aisles of food.

"Hello, Sheriff," Eva said. She smiled briefly at Buck. She took off her hat and shook the water out of it.

"Hey, Eva," Noodles said. "What you been up to? Where's the stump?"

"Pardon?"

"I said, where's old Ed?"

"He's off on a run."

"Left you alone in that old house, has he?"

"I'm all right. I've got Pearl." She smiled at Buck again. Noodles looked at Buck, at Eva, at Buck.

"Hey, boy," he said. "Give me a couple packs of Luckies." He ran his eyes over the shelves of whiskey, which were directly behind the check-out counter. "And give me a bottle of that bourbon, that Ten High." Buck took Noodles' money and put the purchases in a paper bag. "Going to Sacramento," he said, "to have me a party." He tipped his Stetson at Eva and slipped out the front door to the rainy street.

"How'd you get here?" Buck asked.

"We walked. We got a ride part way but we walked most of it."

"In the rain?"

"We wanted to see you." She stepped up to the counter. She leaned over and kissed him; her face was a little wet with rain.

"Hey," he said. "Leo's back there. And the old guys."

"I don't care."

"What?"

"I don't care who sees."

Pearl appeared at the counter. She reached up and dropped four boxes of animal crackers in front of Buck. Eva took off Pearl's bonnet and unbuttoned her rain-coat.

"Pearl's the one who wanted to see you. She had to stock up on cookies."

"Is that all you want, Pearl?" Buck asked.

"Yes."

"That'll be forty cents." Pearl stared at him blankly. He pressed the release button on the cash register, wiggled his fingers in the tray full of coins, then slammed the cash drawer shut. "OK," he said. "They're all yours."

But Pearl didn't seem to have noticed; she was staring down the aisle at the men around the electric heater. She walked to the back of the store and climbed up on an old man's lap. She put an arm around his neck and kissed him noisily on the cheek. He set her down on the floor but she climbed back up. He decided to let her stay; she began bouncing up and down on his lap.

"Listen," Eva said. "I've decided to run away with you."

"You have?"

"Yes." She looked at him directly, boldly. "Is that all right?"

"Well, I don't know. What makes you think I was leaving?"

"But you are, aren't you?"

"I hadn't thought about it. If I was I'd just do it. I wouldn't be running away."

"I've got to get away." Eva was staring at him; Buck felt pinned down by her gaze. "I've decided, I'm through with him. I haven't cared about him in years. I've just been scared to death. It's like living with a crazy man, you're never really relaxed, you don't know what he's going to do. He could do anything when he gets angry. So I've got to leave."

"Just take off, without telling him or anything?"

"Oh, he'll find out soon enough. He wouldn't let me go otherwise. I know him. He gets crazy if things don't go his way. He'd sooner have me dead, than gone off with another man."

Buck nodded. Eva lit a cigarette and inhaled deeply. Leo was walking up to the front of the store to empty the cash register; Buck heard the familiar sound of his shuffling feet.

"I'll go wait in the car," she said. She retrieved Pearl, bundled her up and filled her arms with boxes of animal crackers. They stepped out into the rain.

"What's up, son?" Leo asked. "Did that woman bring you troubles?"

"No."

"Well now, you look troubled." He stepped up to the cash register, released the drawer and began stuffing the loose coins into rolls. He had a smell to him, dried soap and tobacco and denture powder, that Buck had grown to like. It was almost a pleasure, standing next to him; there was the smell, distinct but not oppressive, and there was his presence, a thin stooped body incapable of rapid or violent motion, bundled up in fluffy slippers and a fuzzy brown cardigan that was stained all over and crudely patched at the elbows.

"She's a handsome woman, that Eva Gray. Plenty of men have had thoughts about her. Not me, of course, but a lot of others. Even little Cecil, who was just a boy; I figure that's why he took off this winter. Something to do with her." Leo was counting out the dollar bills now, arranging them in a neat pile. "But she's got a terrible husband. Oh, I don't mean he's a *bad* husband, you understand, I wouldn't know about that"— Leo paused to lick his finger, wrap a rubber band around the ones and begin to count the fives—"What I mean is, he can be a terrible hard, evil man when he gets angry. Why, I was standing here, just like this, one day last fall, standing here with Cecil and Herbie Hartman, who was talking about something or other—let's see, I think he was telling a story on Noodles, Noodles and a nest of hornets, it was awful funny—when in comes Ed Gray, dragging his bad leg along, and walks right up to the counter, right up to here, and smiles at little Cecil, you know sort of a crazy man's smile, and says in the calmest voice, 'Leave her be, sonny. Or I'll shoot your face off.' Said something like that, I don't know if I got it exactly; in the calmest voice, you understand. Then he turns around and stumps on out. And Cecil turned white as a sheet. I believe that's when he decided to spend the winter up in Alturas." Leo wrapped up the fives, picked out the lone twenty and dropped all the money in a canvas sack. He looked searchingly at Buck.

"So you be careful," he said.

"I'm not afraid."

"Now, I didn't say you were."

"I'm not afraid of him. He won't scare me off."

"No, I'm sure he won't."

"He won't try that shit with me." Buck heard his own voice echoing in the quiet store; it sounded loud and dramatic. He thought of something else to say but the words stuck in his throat.

Leo shrugged his shoulders. He tied up the canvas sack and shut the cash register. He shuffled off to the back of the store.

They drove back home through the light rain. Pearl sat between them in the front seat of Buck's Chevy, her mouth full of animal crackers. She would chew a bunch until they merged in a ball of gooey dough. Then she would take the ball in her hand and play with it. She made pancakes and doughnuts and little statues of indeterminate shape. Her hands were soon covered with the stuff; she wiped them off on the car seat.

The countryside looked grayer and more dismal to Buck now than ever before. The soft drizzle made the dark sky and the uninterrupted flat fields melt together, so that the straight two-lane road seemed to float without any firm contacts in an ocean of misty gray space. He was having trouble seeing the road; once he lost it entirely, and was guided back by the sound of his tires hissing on wet pavement. A huge semi came thundering down out of nowhere; it sprayed muddy water all over the windshield and its concussion almost knocked the Chevy off the road. Buck heard Eva gasp and he saw her put a protective arm around Pearl, who was still busy with the crackers. He thought of Ed Gray, driving just such a huge truck somewhere down south, his bad leg jamming the gas to the floor and his thick, viper-tattooed arm wrestling with the wheel. It would be easy to bully cars in a rig like that, they would look so small and annoying, like bees; you would hardly feel it when you rammed them off the road.

"Listen," Eva said. She was looking out the windshield at the rain. "If you don't want to take me, just say so. Maybe it's a bad idea."

"No."

"I can figure something out on my own. You don't have to get mixed up in it."

"No, I want to be mixed up."

"You see I'm sick of this. Sticking to a crazy man, like

I was his slave. You know what he's like? He's sick, really sick in the head. He don't need me, he needs a doctor. He never wants to talk or do anything, except drink and sit or drive his truck. And he is something to see in bed, let me tell you. He's got some strange ideas."

"Like what?"

"I don't want to talk about it."

They passed the grove of oak trees and pulled into the muddy driveway. The car stopped and Pearl climbed over Eva and ran up to the front door, which was never locked, and disappeared inside. Eva slid along the car seat until she was right next to Buck. They kissed.

"I mean it," she said. "I don't want you mixed up in it, less you really want to be. I could go away and then you could come and meet me somewheres."

"No," he said. "We'll do it together."

"You sure?"

"I sure am." She put her arms around him and buried her face in his neck. He felt suddenly protective and fatherly. It was a nice feeling; he smiled to himself and stroked her arm. The car was cozy and quiet. He pushed Ed Gray out of his thoughts. He would worry about him later; there was plenty of time, he would figure something out.

"Buck," Eva said. It was not a question, or the preface to a question; it was just his name. It had a wonderful sound, coming from her, from her long throat, in her rich woman's voice. It filled him with warmth; he felt loved, he felt powerful and complete. He pressed her against the car seat and kissed her until they both lost their breath. Then they sat for a while in the warm car, listening to the rain natter against the metal roof.

VIII

Eva wanted to leave immediately. She packed a suitcase with her essential things and hid it in a closet. Ed was due back on Sunday, and she wanted to go before she saw him again, not because she would feel bad when she saw him, guilty about leaving him, but because he would scare her, just by being himself, silent and sour, and she was through being scared. But Buck thought they ought to wait, at least for a while. Let Ed come back and loaf for a couple of days; he'd be gone soon enough on another trip, and then they could take off. It would be two weeks before he found out they were gone, and they would have time to get good and lost. Eva finally agreed, his was a better plan. She left the packed suitcase in the closet so they could get away quickly when the time came.

Eva needed a lot of comforting now. She was pale again and preoccupied. She sat in the kitchen reading or just staring, lighting cigarettes and then forgetting them, so that they burned little furrows around the edge of the table. Sometimes she stared at nothing for half an hour and then suddenly got up and sat on Buck's lap and curled up against him, just like Pearl. He would hold her and pat her on the back, and then, inevitably, he would get excited feeling her weight and her spreading softness through the smooth fabric of her housecoat. They would walk upstairs, arms around each other, and get in bed.

They made love over and over again, as if trying to get it right through practice. Eva was full of excitement, nervous as well as sexual; sometimes she was slippery between the legs before they had their clothes off. Then sometimes she broke out in ticklish laughter just as Buck was giving her what he thought to be a tender caress. He would slow down and lighten his pressure, but it was no use, she couldn't be touched then; just seeing or feeling him nearby sent her into gales of hysterical laughter. So they would separate for a while; she wouldn't let herself even look at him. And in a few minutes it was all right; they came together again like magnets, like crashing cars, like meshing gears, like bodies.

He was a little amazed at himself. This much sex, again and again, was new in his limited experience. After a certain point he didn't know where the erections came from, but there they were, or there it was, a little swollen and insensitive from overuse but eager and hungry for Eva. Sometimes he stood outside himself and marveled at his body, at its persistence; it was following orders he wasn't aware of giving; it seemed to have another mind, autonomous and just as powerful as the one he was thinking with.

Something like that had been happening all his life: another mind spoke up suddenly, and the rest of him went along, only vaguely aware of what was taking place. That was what had happened in the city, it seemed like years ago, when he started his troubles; it was what had happened with Eva, when he agreed to run away. Things just happened, there were no laws and there was no question of being in control; they happened. The rest of you was aware or not aware, or maybe even slightly amused. You watched, you might be amazed at how powerful and definite your voice was, you chose this over that with such certainty it seemed you must have thought it through carefully, when actually it was all a surprise. He surprised himself often; he kept waking up to himself in starts.

Everything was more or less like that, he was convinced; things were not in control. They always turned out differently from what you had expected, more bizarre or less bizarre, with a final shape you could never have predicted. Take this whole thing with Eva; he remembered how she had been when he saw her two months ago, cold and deathlike in the flickering blue light of Ed's TV; how could he have predicted the film of sweat that was gluing their bodies together now, or the fish-and-ammonia smell of their tired bed? No, there was no predicting things and there were no laws, Buck was certain of that.

And he felt pretty good with things that way. He felt free. Nothing was very serious; you could do just about what you wanted. Acts didn't seem to have consequences, or if they did, they were almost impossible to discover. It was hard enough keeping track of all that was going on in the present; he really couldn't think very well about what might happen some time way in the future. The future was such a grand canyon, you got dizzy looking in it. Anything, really anything at all could happen; you could make an escape from anywhere, given enough time.

So he wasn't particularly worried, waiting to leave. But Eva got more and more anxious; she smoked and stared and looked like she would crack her forehead with all her furrowing. She got him to stay home from work Friday and keep her company; they spent the day in bed. Pearl roamed the downstairs happily, scattering animal crackers all over and trying to feed them to the spiders she trapped in the basement. She was a little lonely when Buck and Eva locked themselves in the upstairs room and stayed there for hours. When they came out she would leap on them, punching and hugging and hopping, a little crazy with the fun of making contact.

On Saturday morning they slept late. Eva woke up first and stared at the dingy ceiling of the room. She watched Buck; he was sleeping on his side with his mouth open and his eyes vibrating under the lids. She slid silently down in the bed and took his cock gently in her mouth. She licked and sucked softly; he stayed asleep for another minute or so, dreaming of a large white house, Spanish-style, filled with people dancing.

Just as Buck woke up, opening his eyes and forgetting his dream in the same instant, so that he began the day feeling baffled; just at that moment, Ed Gray was driving through the empty intersection of highways five and seven, just south of Yarbee and six miles away from his house. He was coming home a day early; he had been fired from his job because of two unreported collisions with slow-moving sedans. As a result of one of the accidents Navaho Truck was being sued for a quarter of a million dollars, and Ed's dispatcher had told him he would never again drive a truck anywhere in the West. Ed was not in a good mood.

He thought briefly of Eva, saw her sitting in the kitchen of their house, waiting for him. He wasn't eager to see her, he wasn't ever very eager but especially not now, when he had just been fired. How would he explain it? And what would they do for money? It made him furious, the whole thing; fired in a minute, and after what, twelve years spreading his ass on the seats of their trucks. There were other accidents he hadn't reported, plenty of accidents, and no one had ever said a word. It went with driving a truck; you had to get your load delivered fast, any way you could do it; you didn't tiptoe around, you drove it like a train.

Driving through Yarbee he passed Zinger's Oasis and thought about stopping for a beer. But the neon Budweiser signs were off; it was too early yet, maybe he'd come back later. It was raining a little, the town looked empty and dismal; as Ed left Yarbee he wondered why he was going home at all. He felt pretty low and there was nothing waiting for him there, only nervous Eva in her smelly housecoat, with her sour tobacco breath. Sometimes she was so scared, so jumpy and terrified that he just wanted to hit her, hard; give her a taste of the real thing; drive out that crazy terror, that woman in her who was always just about to scream. She was worse now than ever; she was crazier and always tight as a wire. Women were like that—they got worse as they got older. They went either of two ways: they got fat and ugly, with the meat hanging out all over, salami tits and huge waffled butts; or else they got crazy. Thinking about Eva made him mad. If she gave him shit about the job, he would hit her some.

Or maybe he should turn around, right now, and leave her for good. There was nothing between them, nothing that tied them together anymore. No kids, and how could there be: her cunt was as cold as a tomb. It was years since he had stuck it in there, Ed thought, and he never much wanted to again. Some women were like that. You stuck it in and they turned to ice, and you felt like they were going to freeze your dick and break it off. They had coffins between their legs, cold, dry coffins that killed off your come, sucked it out and then froze it to death, and would kill the rest of you, too, if you didn't wise up. No, there was nothing tying him to Eva. He would see how things went; he'd tell her about the job, see how she reacted. If he felt like it, he'd leave her cold.

He passed a new Ford pickup going the other way; he recognized Moon and Freddy Cargo in it but he didn't wave. As he was driving by a deserted-looking farmhouse three miles from his own, Buck was rolling on top of Eva and planting himself inside her; they fit together nicely, in a by-now accustomed position. Eva's knees were drawn up to cradle his body, and her heels rested on his buttocks; her hands roamed over his back and her neck craned forward so that she could watch the tangled reflection they made in the long, warped mirror across the room. Ed drove on; he switched on his windshield wipers as the drizzle turned to rain. One of his ears popped suddenly and began to buzz. He shook his head violently. He slapped a hand against the ear, then stuck a finger in and scoured it around. But the sound continued, now turning into a high-pitched whistle.

He drove on. The asphalt highway was shiny and slippery in the rain. Eva was digging her fingernails into Buck's shoulders. He pressed harder and humped faster; he took her small pink ear in his mouth and began breathing hoarsely. Her eyes were wide open as she examined their reflection. They were a huge animal, a four-legged something; Buck's balls in their wrinkled sack were bouncing and trembling with every thrust.

She started to come and she watched herself push a finger in his hole just as Ed, driven to distraction by the chorus of whistles now in both of his ears, turned into the muddy driveway and switched off his car. He pounded the top of his balding head several times trying to drive out the noises. He gritted his teeth and cursed silently. As he slid out of the car he cracked the point of his elbow against the steering wheel. His funny bone vibrated like a tuning fork; he groaned audibly. Buck and Eva moaned and gasped and came together, a first for them, their insides joined in a long delicious spasm. They soon fell apart and began to doze.

Ed walked in the front door and shut it behind him. He expected to see Eva in the kitchen, smoking and reading, but she wasn't there. The house looked deserted, in fact. The lights were all off and it was chilly inside. The living room was very neat, except for an empty box of animal crackers on the hassock; it looked as if someone had straightened up, turned off the lights and the heat and then left. He walked into the yellow kitchen. It was empty and clean. There weren't any dirty breakfast dishes around; even the ashtrays were clean.

He went back to the cold living room. The drapes were drawn, it was dark as night with the lights off and the rainy day outside. He walked to the foot of the stairs and listened: the house was silent. He took a couple of steps up and then he heard a noise, a clattering. He froze. He didn't know why, but he was a little spooked in the empty house; he heard another noise and he whirled around, bringing his hands up to his chest; he waited, stock-still on the stairs, holding his breath and staring in the direction of the kitchen. Then Pearl walked into the living room, beautiful little Pearl, saw him standing there and stopped. She stared at him blankly. Ed breathed with relief and walked down to greet her.

"Pearl. You scared me to death, little girl." She put her arms around him and he picked her up, swung her from side to side, then set her down. She grabbed hold of his belt. "How are you, Pearl?" he said. She stared up at him. He stroked her silky hair and smiled at her.

"Where is everybody?" he asked. She said nothing. "Where's your mommy and daddy?" She stared at him; then she frowned and her face crinkled up. He patted her head; "Don't cry," he said. "Did they leave you behind?" He sat down heavily in his favorite chair. He kicked the cookie box off the hassock and laid his bad leg out. His hand automatically fell to the floor, searching for a can of beer. Pearl straddled his outstretched leg, walked along it, then curled up in his lap. She kissed his face. He put an arm around her and bounced her up and down, like a department-store Santa Claus.

"Where's Eva?" Pearl didn't seem to have heard; she was pressing her small fists against his belly. "Gone and left you, has she? God." He looked around the living room again. With the TV off it looked terribly dark and empty, a spooky place to leave a little girl. "That bitch," he said. Pearl looked him in the face for a second; then she looked down at his belly and started to rub it.

Ed sat back and relaxed. No one seemed to be around, and that was just as well. He hadn't looked forward to seeing Eva and telling her about his job; now he could forget about it for a while. Pearl was bouncing on his lap and stroking his belly. It felt good. She was a good kid, even if she was retarded, or whatever; he would be glad to have her as his daughter, she was beautiful and affectionate. She liked to touch. He sat back and let her do what she wanted, let her stroke his belly and his chest, even his thighs and between his legs. She kissed him, rapidly, his forehead and his cheeks and his mouth, kissing his big face round and round in a circle. It felt funny, like a swarm of bees on his face. He closed his eyes and let her go ahead, around and around and around; after a while it started to tickle and he had to laugh.

Suddenly he pushed her away and sat up. He had heard something. He looked quickly to either side and strained his ears; he thought he had heard something again, upstairs. But soon it was gone; even the buzzing in his ears was gone. The house was dark and empty, he was finally convinced. He relaxed again. Pearl lay full length against his reclining body. She pressed her face against his chest and wriggled the rest of her like a weasel. Ed closed his eyes and breathed deeply through his mouth. His hand came up and patted her on the head, on the back, on her small behind; his hand slipped under her short pleated skirt and felt the smooth skin on the backs of her thighs, and the slightly rounded silkiness of her panties. Her behind fit like a grapefruit in his hand; he squeezed it gently, he felt for the shallow crack and followed it with his finger.

Pearl's legs fell apart and she sat up. She sat astride his outstretched leg for a minute and then stood up. She looked blankly at Ed. He reached out and took one of her hands. He stood up, a little clumsy with his wooden limb; it stuck out awkwardly, it was unusually hard to control. Pearl touched it. She led him out of the living room and through the kitchen. They opened the cellar door and walked slowly down the dark stairs. Ed was blind; he held on tightly to Pearl's little hand. Once he slipped and grabbed for the banister just in time. Pearl waited a moment, then led him the rest of the way down.

They walked across the dark cellar. Ed could barely see. It was cold and unusually damp from all the rain, but he didn't notice. The ringing was back in his ears, loud and eerie, as loud as a whistle. He felt something soft under his feet; Pearl lay down in the pile of rags, and her hand pulled him down. He bent over, he stooped, finally he fell, face down in the rags.

He held her loose body against him. She felt small and incredibly light, like a doll. He put his face against her hair; her head was warm and her hair was fragrant, it had a simple child's smell, young skin and oil and soap. It was a wonderful smell. Ed buried his face in her hair. He rubbed his face from side to side, inhaling deeply; he couldn't get enough of her fragrance, it was wonderful, it was magical. He wrapped his thighs around her slender body and held her tight against him. He could see her face dimly now; it was blank and her eyes were open. He pulled her panties down her legs and gently felt her smooth groin. He laid her on her back, lifted her skirt and looked at her. He spread her legs apart and kissed her there, a long soft kiss, a tender kiss, the most tender he ever gave.

He opened his fly and pulled out his member. It was hard and achingly full; it was as big as her arm. "Touch it," he said, but Pearl kept still. "Touch it," he said again. His ears were ringing with sound, it was deafening, he felt dizzy with the loudness of it. He slid Pearl's body down, opened her mouth with his fingers and fit her on him. Then he came, with a violent jerking and bursting.

He woke up; Pearl was gagging against the rags. It sounded as if she was choking to death. He pounded her on the back and cleaned out her mouth with a finger. He picked up a rag and wiped off her face. There was a ringing in his ears like bells, heavy clanging bells; he felt as if his head would split. Pearl lay back and watched him silently while he searched for her panties. They had disappeared in the rag pile and he was throwing rags everywhere now, burrowing like a mole. He was suddenly terrified. He had to find her panties, he was frantic, he had to find her panties or he was all through. That was the message in his head, the message of all the ringing bells and deafening whistles; he had to find her panties. He found them and hurriedly pulled them on her. Then he stood up. He stared down at Pearl; she was lying perfectly still in the pile of rags, staring back at him. He looked at her for a minute, then stumped rapidly across the cellar and up the flight of stairs. He walked quickly through the kitchen and into the living room. He looked all around; an empty box of animal crackers was lying in the middle of the floor. The house was dark and quiet; it was empty, Ed Gray thought. There was nothing of his around, nothing to show he had come back. The noises were cascading in his ear, they sounded like hundreds of police cars, ambulances and fire engines—a stampede of vehicles, all in his pursuit. He shut the front door behind him. He limped as quickly as he could down the muddy drive. He pulled out onto highway seven and speeded off, driving anywhere far away.

IX

Eva woke up to a sound from downstairs, a door closing or something falling on the floor. She felt groggy and a little worthless; she had slept into the early afternoon, for no other reason than that her bed was warm and the world was cold. Buck felt her stirring and woke up too. He had had some amazing dreams, he said, but now he couldn't remember them.

They took a shower and went downstairs. The house was dark and chilly; Buck stumbled over the hassock before Eva found the light switch and turned it on. She turned up the heat, then went in the kitchen and put on a pot of coffee. Pearl walked up from the basement and stood next to her at the stove.

"Hello, honey," Eva said. She dropped two slices of bread in the toaster. Pearl stood next to her like a statue; once she wiped her mouth with the back of her hand. Eva looked at her closely.

"What's the matter, Pearl? Are you mad cause we stayed in bed?" She put an arm around Pearl and gave her a hug. She kissed her on the top of the head. Then she held her at arm's length. "What's the matter?" she asked.

Pearl opened her mouth wide, then shut it. She screwed up her face, suddenly began to cry, then just as suddenly stopped and looked blank again. "He," she said.

"Who?"

"He," she said. She gave Eva an agitated look; she

grunted once, then shook her head so that her yellow hair flew from side to side.

"Who is he?" Eva asked.

Pearl shook her head some more. "Made me," she said. Her face strained around some words she couldn't say; she closed her eyes and grimaced, and looked like she was going to scream. Then her face relaxed completely. Eva kissed her forehead and hugged her firmly.

"It's all right," she said. "I bet you miss your ma, don't you? Don't you, Pearl? Well, she's coming back real soon."

Buck walked into the kitchen. "The toast," he said. There were two little columns of smoke floating up; Eva dropped Pearl and rescued the toast, just in time. They all ate a simple breakfast. Buck was unusually hungry and he drank a lot of coffee; he was wide awake and full of energy for the rest of the day.

They stayed at home all Saturday and then all Sunday, waiting for Ed to come back. Eva was calmer than she had been for several days; she was ready now, her fear was under control and she was armed with the certainty that within four or five days she would be leaving both Ed and his dismal house for good. But Ed didn't show. They sat around all day and evening in postures of innocent domesticity, expecting him to come at any minute; the upstairs bed was neatly made with fresh new sheets, and Eva had taken the precaution of ruffling up Ed's double bed so it looked used. But nothing happened.

Just after dark on Sunday a truck pulled in the drive. It was Herbie and Nancy Hartman, back from Redding with many stories of their aunt Ida and a large plastic doll for Pearl, a doll who spoke when a certain string was pulled and who wet her tiny underpants whenever she was laid on her back. Pearl was only mildly interested in the doll; she said nothing to her parents but soon climbed up on Nancy's lap and held her tightly around the neck. She refused to walk to the truck when the Hartmans left; her arms were locked around her mother's neck and could not be loosened.

Eva was dying to tell her sister about the plan. She almost blurted it out once but caught herself in time. Buck had said not to tell anyone; then Ed couldn't pressure them to spill the beans. Still, it was hard not telling Nancy. She promised herself she would write as soon as they were safely away, so that Nancy wouldn't worry. She couldn't wait until she could write that letter. She was composing it in her head as the Hartmans walked to their pickup, Nancy wearing a blank-faced Pearl like a fifty-pound necklace, and Herbie holding the talented new doll by an ankle upside down; "Dearest sister," it went, "We are safe and far away. . . . I tried and tried but I couldn't help it—I have fallen in love with a wonderful man. . . ."

Monday morning Buck went in to work. He rushed home as soon as the store closed, at five; he found Eva reading Luke Short in the kitchen and a spaghetti dinner simmering on the stove. She had fixed the spaghetti, Ed's favorite, to welcome him back, but since there was still no sign of him she served it up to Buck. It was unlike Ed to be late, she said. The truck schedules were usually very exact; he almost always came back the day he said he would. They waited. Buck worked Tuesday and again came home to find Eva alone, stirring a large pot of chili con carne on the stove. Chili was Ed's second favorite; they ate it in silence, and then, sitting around the table feeling stuffed, they decided they were going to leave, regardless of what Ed was doing. Eva jumped up to go get her suitcase but Buck stopped her. He felt fat and full, and his face was covered with brown chili stains; he didn't like traveling at night, he said, so why didn't they wait just a few more hours and leave Wednesday morning, after a good sleep? So it was finally decided; they were going to leave tomorrow. They kissed each other good night and went off to sleep in their separate bedrooms.

X

Late Tuesday night, just as Eva was falling asleep and Buck, unable to sleep, was staring into the darkness of his room, listening to the creaking and the moaning of the old wooden house, Sheriff Noodles Pisco was driving his squad car south out of Sacramento, bound for Royo County and home. He took the busy interstate highway for a few miles and then exited onto a parallel road, a deserted old two-lane road where it was unlikely that he would be seen.

Noodles was as confused as he had ever been in his life. Strange voices and odd phrases kept playing through his head, voices he had heard in the course of the weekend. He would listen to one, repeating the words over and over to himself, slowly; but instead of getting clearer the words got more and more senseless, like words in a foreign language. "A certain obligation"—that's what a little man had said to him, a little man with a rat face and the tiniest gray mustache over a smiling mouth—"You have a certain obligation, Mr.

Pisco; I done you a favor or two, Mr. Pisco, and now you got to me a certain obligation." Obligation obligation—now, what was an obligation? Noodles thought he knew, but the more he said it, mouthing the word to himself over and over inside the cold squad car, the more it sounded crazy, like a magic word or a spell— "obla obla, obligation, a certain obla obla. . . ."

He lit another cigarette and stuck it in his mouth. It tasted terrible but he smoked hungrily; it felt as if he had been smoking the same hot, harsh cigarette all weekend. He had gone up to Sacramento expecting a good time, just wanting to get laid, but instead there was the little man, Joe Candy—"My name is Joe Candy, you can call me Mr. Candy"—waiting for him with a big smile and a piece of advice: "You got to me a certain obligation, Mr. Pisco, we don't want no trouble and you don't want no trouble; we got some little favors you could do us, Mr. Pisco, Mr. Piss-go, Mr. Sheriff. . . ." And then there was the letter, on crumpled yellow paper, that Mr. Candy had pulled out of his vest pocket and given him to read; he had read it over and over, not quite believing the few words written in light pencil, faded words you had to strain your eyes to see: "Dear husband, We are safe and alive. Marcus has got real big. I love you no matter what. I love you. Lilian   PS: Do what this man says and we are alive some more." He had read the letter until Mr. Candy plucked it out of his fingers and stuffed it back in his vest pocket. "A nice lady," he had said, smiling and wrinkling his long nose, smiling so hard his mustache disappeared. "You want her back, Mr. Piss-go? It can be done, it can be done. . . ."

Noodles drove on, smoking and muttering to himself.

The road was wet from the recent rain, and outside it was cold and black. " 'It can be done,' " he was saying to himself, " 'it can be done' "; just what, he was thinking, did they want him to do? Candy had given him a list of county documents he wanted, deeds and bills of sale, that sort of thing. It would be easy enough to get them, Noodles thought, but why? What was going on? "I am a businessman like any other," Candy had said. "And you have got to me a certain obligation. A certain obligation, Mr. Piss-go; you don't want and we don't want; a certain, Mr. Piss-go, a certain can be done. . . ."

Noodles lit a fresh cigarette. The little pack of Luckies in his shirt pocket looked like a square nipple on the huge swell of his chest. There was an AM receiver built into his police radio; he switched it on but all he could get was a Spanish-speaking station, coming in faintly through the static. He turned the radio off. His mind was full of mysterious words and pictures; he saw Mr. Candy and all the whores, a blonde who had showed him a certain trick you could do with a rubber horseshoe, and a redhead with a big ass, and the one with long hair, the angry one who looked like Lilian. He tried to think of Lilian, his wife, but all he could see was the face of the angry whore. My God, he's got Lilian somewhere, Noodles thought; his throat choked up and his eyes began to burn, and he would have cried but for the fact that he was the county sheriff, driving home in a high-powered squad car.

It began to rain again, very lightly. It was more like dew than rain, and Noodles had to turn the wipers off every few minutes, when the windshield began to squeak. He was only twenty miles from Royo County;

he began looking for the cutoff road that would take him across the interstate to highway seven. He thought of dapper Mr. Candy, sitting at one of the back tables in his plush "restaurant," flanked by two brutal-looking bodyguards, two Negroes in sharkskin suits; he thought of Lilian, who had disappeared more than a year ago —was she one of Candy's whores now, her fine long legs spread wide to the whole world? And he thought of Marcus, his melon-headed son who had disappeared along with Lilian; maybe he was still alive, growing abnormally fast like all the Piscos, but scared to death by what was going on around him, the garish whores with their red-faced johns, big black thugs, beatings, murders, dope-pushing and who knew what else. Noodles groaned loudly. The sound of his own voice in the speeding car startled him. He stubbed out his cigarette and lit another.

A new Chevy sedan full of people passed him, going the other way, but Noodles was too preoccupied to notice. It was an outlandish car; its two gleaming carburetors stuck up through holes that had been cut in the hood, and the sleek chassis stood high above the frame, raised by means of spacers in the springs. The Chevy stopped suddenly and executed a skidding U-turn on the slick narrow road. It caught up with the squad car and began to follow at a distance of fifty yards.

Noodles saw the Chevy in his rear-view mirror. He slowed down slightly and tried to compose himself for the benefit of the people in the other car; he leaned way back in his seat, in a posture both casual and authoritative; he wiped the anxious look off his face and replaced it with a confident smile. But Mr. Candy and his enigmatic words haunted him, and he soon forgot about the following car. What was he going to do? Candy was some sort of crook, Noodles could see that. But what could be done? The crook had him over a barrel; he had Lilian somewhere, maybe, and little Marcus. And then there were those nights with the whores; it wouldn't be good to let that get known. Noodles couldn't help smiling when he thought about the whores, all the nasty things they had let him do. Maybe Candy had made tapes or movies of those little parties; Noodles giggled excitedly at the thought of what they would look like.

He stopped giggling; the Chevy behind him had switched on its brights, and the reflection in the rear-view was hurting his eyes. He glanced over the back seat. The Chevy was close, maybe twenty yards away. The car looked full, there were four men in the front seat, and one of them was leaning out of the window on the shotgun side. It looked like he was waving or shaking his fist, but Noodles couldn't be sure in the blaze of the headlights. He speeded up. He could stop and give them a ticket, but he wasn't in the mood; anyway he was still outside the county. Their lights were blinding him. He squinted and tilted his rear-view so that it didn't reflect.

"You got to me a certain obligation." Noodles shivered as he remembered Mr. Candy's words and his ratlike face. There was something very frightening about the little man, and it wasn't just his mean-looking black bodyguards in their sharkskin suits. They had looked capable of anything, anything vicious and painful, but they had been unmistakably in Mr. Candy's control. He was just a little skinny man, almost a midget; he spoke softly and gestured freely with his tiny pink hands; for a second you thought of laughing in his face but in the next second you were scared, chilled, speechless. His voice was soft and a little bored; you got the feeling that he was never disobeyed, that he was used to ordering anything, a pepperoni pizza or a death, in that same tone of voice, soft and dignified and slightly bored.

Noodles shivered in his cold squad car. He threw away his half-smoked cigarette and lit another. He wasn't ready to die, he decided, and he wasn't about to abandon his son or let his wife get fucked to death. As he took the cutoff over to highway seven he had just about decided: he would get Candy his papers and then call it quits. He would stop seeing the whores, and he would demand that they give him back his wife. And what did they want with all those documents anyway? What could you do just with papers? Candy was a crook but there was nothing to steal in Royo County; all there was, was land, flat land, worthless to everyone but a few farmers, and not worth much to them. Noodles felt better. He passed over the busy interstate. When he crossed the county line he had decided definitely to do it. He opened his window a crack to let in some fresh air. He was almost pleased with himself; he felt much better.

The Chevy followed him across the overpass and into Royo County. The lights of the interstate soon faded, and the two cars sped down the narrow black stripe of highway seven. Noodles readjusted his mirror and squinted at the Chevy. They were right on his tail, not ten yards away; he speeded up, he slowed down, he gunned his car to ninety and still the Chevy dogged him. Noodles was getting mad. He was in his own county now, and he was in charge; nobody could give him shit in Royo County. Especially not a bunch of hoods, or, what was more likely, a bunch of greasers, drunk greasers. He pushed his Ford up to a hundred, then a hundred and ten; suddenly he slammed on his brakes, and the Chevy, braking just an instant late, collided with his rear end and bounced off. Noodles heard glass breaking and smiled to himself. He switched on his bright red revolving dome light. He put his arm out the window and signaled; he pulled off the highway and drove a few yards into a fallow field. The Chevy followed obediently.

Noodles reached for the ticket book that was clipped to his sun visor. Then he climbed slowly out of his Ford. He was almost smiling as he walked toward the Chevy; he walked slowly, with a rolling, confident gait. He stopped between the cars, he stood for a moment with hand on hip in the light of the Chevy's one remaining headlight. He saw the broken taillight on his squad car; he shook his head in disgust and wrote something in his ticket book. He sauntered up to the driver's window. He stood a foot or two away; he took a long look at the Chevy, at the oversized racing tires, the de-chromed and refinished body, the gleaming carburetors nosing through the hood. He shook his head again and spat on the ground. He could smell the beer inside the car.

He put his hands on his hips, bent over and stuck out his jaw. He looked at the boy in the driver's seat. "You dumb greaser," he said. "You got yourself in big trouble now. Real big trouble."

"No," the driver said impassively. Noodles heard

metal clanking against metal. He looked up. A man on the other side of the car was resting the barrels of a shotgun across the roof. The shotgun was aimed at Noodles' face.

The four doors of the car opened and the eight young men got out. They were all of medium height; they looked identical in the dark. Someone slipped Noodles' pistols out of their tooled leather holsters. The man with the shotgun walked around the front of the car and stood just in front of Noodles, the barrels of the gun pointing up at his broad face. Someone fished in his pocket and pulled out his key ring; the keys jingled like bells while the man searched for the right one. Noodles' handcuffs were removed from his belt and used to lock his hands behind his back. A man grabbed his shirt front and led him around behind the cars.

No one spoke. Noodles jerked his head all around, from dark face to dark face. His eyes and his mouth were wide open in fright and surprise. Someone tripped him and he fell face down, without his arms to protect him; his wind escaped in a loud grunt. A man sat on his back while two others bent up his legs and hogtied his handcuffed wrists to his ankles. His face was buried in the wet dirt; he had to crane his neck painfully to breathe. His legs felt as if they were about to snap in half. "Wait," he said in a strangled voice. "No, wait," he said.

A man crouched in front of his head and lifted it up by the hair. Noodles couldn't make out his face in the dark but he could smell the man's sweat and his beer breath. The man leaned way down so that their faces were close enough to kiss. "For Luiz," he said. "And the others."

"Wait," Noodles said. The man let go and Noodles' face dropped into the dirt. The eight men stood around his huge body. He was enormous, even tied up and lying on the ground. Then they were kicking him, first tentatively and then harder. They stood around him in a circle and kicked. His body jerked a little with each blow; they were standing at his sides and at his legs and at his head, kicking with great force. No one spoke. Soon they were sweating and grunting with the force of their work. One man kicked too hard and fell, full length, across Noodles' body; he gasped and scrambled up, and rubbed his chest as if it had touched fire.

They kicked him, standing all around. Some of the men stepped back a foot or two and then hopped forward, kicking with extra momentum. Their boots against his body made a soft thudding sound, like dough being punched or a carpet being beaten; there was no sound of breaking bones. The waning moon suddenly broke through the ceiling of clouds and lit everything up, the cars, the eight men, the edge of a nearby canal, the huge lump of Noodles' body, and the wet earth; everything glowed silver for a moment. The men stopped and looked, they were breathing heavily. Then the clouds closed up and it was dark again. They kicked as hard as they could. His body was slack now and it gave freely with every kick. His body was huge, incredibly huge, a bull's body, enormously wide and nearly as high as their waists. They kicked, feeling their feet small against the great volume of his body. They kicked and kicked and something very tiny snapped inside his huge body. Then they kicked until their feet were sore and they were exhausted. They stood around his body, gasping for air.

A man crouched down and lifted Noodles' head. He stared into the startled face and then laid it softly against the ground. He pointed toward the canal and four of the men tried to pick Noodles up by the arms and legs, but it couldn't be done; the connections in his body were broken, his limbs felt like they would rip away. They left him where he was lying. Seven of the men quickly piled into the Chevy. The engine started and the car backed off to the highway. The eighth man took the gas cap off the squad car and stuck a twisted cloth down the pipe. He lit the end of the cloth and ran. As the Chevy pulled away the squad car exploded in a tower of red and orange flame. The whole night was lit up; even the low clouds caught the brilliance of the fire, and turned pink and red and orange for an hour.

XI

Toward morning the clouds began to break up. The rain stopped completely and the flat fields dried out with amazing speed. The rainwater that had collected in the irrigation ditches began to disappear; if you had sat at the edge of one of the canals that morning, you would have seen the water level slowly lower, like water draining out of a tub. In a matter of hours the water was all gone; all that remained in the canals was a thick layer of red mud.

The clouds broke up but didn't disappear. They scattered and spun themselves into long white cottony shreds and made a sort of loose net over the sky. The sun shone through now and again; the clouds seemed uncertain whether to break up for good, or to come together again in a dense gray ceiling.

Just after eight in the morning a late-model electric blue Pontiac exited off the interstate freeway and onto Royo County highway seven. It was a well-kept, conservative-looking car; it drove slowly down the deserted two-lane road, through puddles that had collected on the blacktop and through patches of sunshine and shade. There were two men in the Pontiac. They were black men, in their forties; they were dressed in neatly pressed dark suits, crisp white shirts and ties. They looked like businessmen, except that they were unusually large and muscular. The driver had a squashed nose and scars around his eyes; his hands were thick and arthritic, like a farmer's or a boxer's. The other man wore sunglasses and a gray felt hat. They said nothing as they drove the first few miles into Royo County.

"Hey," said the man in the hat. He pointed out his window; just a few yards off the road was the black husk of a burned-out car. "Stop," he said.

"What for?"

"Just stop." The driver pulled over and the other man hopped out. He walked quickly up to the car. There was steam rising from the body, and it was warm to the touch. It had a strong smell—burnt paint and plastic, burnt gasoline and the half-burnt stuffing of the seats. Mounted vertically on the blackened dash was a long-barreled shotgun; the wooden stock had been burned away.

He stuck his head carefully through a window whose glass had melted down. It was still hot in the car; everything had been destroyed, cracked or melted or incinerated. It smelled terrible. He pulled his head out, taking care not to dirty his hat. The metal of the body had buckled at certain points. The red dome light on the roof had melted into a firm puddle of shapeless plastic. He walked slowly around the car, brushing off the sleeves of his suit coat and shooting his cuffs. He saw the body of the sheriff lying a few yards away. Parts of his clothing had ignited from the intense heat, and the flesh underneath was burned black. The man in the gray hat stared for a moment into the face of the dead sheriff. Then he walked quickly down to the Pontiac.

They pulled slowly away. "Guess what," said the man in the hat. He was breathing audibly.

"What?"

"We don't have to worry about the heat."

"Why not?"

"Cause it's dead."

They drove on, slowly. They drove past a few farmhouses and barns. Once they overtook and passed an old pickup. The sun shone brightly for a while and then disappeared behind some clouds. They pulled into the little town of Yarbee. The main street was empty. They drove nearly to the end of town and parked across the street from the general store. There was a gas pump in front of the store. The man with a squashed nose looked absentmindedly at his gas gauge; it read full.

He watched as the man in the hat got out of the Pontiac and strode purposefully across the wide street. When he was a few yards away the sun suddenly burst out from behind the clouds and lit the town up brilliantly. The man in the hat looked up at the sky and pressed his sunglasses more firmly against his nose. He walked to the door of the general store and tried it; it was locked. He knocked firmly. He peered in through the stained and dusty front window of the store. He pounded loudly with his fist.

An old man came to the door. He was wearing baggy flannel pants over a suit of longjohns; as he stood there in the doorway, shading his eyes from the bright sunlight, he leaned this way and that, reaching for his galluses and looping them over his narrow shoulders. From across the street the man in the Pontiac watched as the man in the gray hat talked and gestured. The old man listened; he stared up at the tall black man. Then he shook his head. The man in the hat talked and gestured some more; the old man stared and shook his head.

The driver watched impassively as the man in the hat looked once to his right and once to his left and then punched the old man in the stomach. He doubled up and fell to his knees; the man in the hat lifted him up, held his face in a large black hand and suddenly punched him again, right in the stomach. The old man fell again. His body shook and it looked as if he spit on the ground. The man in the hat reached down and grabbed a handful of gray hair. He jerked the old man's head up; then he bent way over and put an ear to the old man's mouth.

The driver watched as the man in hat and sunglasses walked back across the street. He got in the Pontiac and they drove quickly out of Yarbee.

"Dead ahead," he said. He ran a finger under his tight collar and shot his cuffs. "Just a few miles," he said. "I'll tell you when."

Buck and Eva were just getting out of bed as the

blue Pontiac pulled into the grove of young oaks by the entrance to the drive. The black men parked the Pontiac; they sat in the car, well hidden by the tree trunks and the shadows. Eva brewed some coffee and fried the last six eggs in the refrigerator. They ate sitting side by side at the kitchen table. Buck kept a hand on Eva's warm leg.

"I can't believe it," she said. There was a pool of egg yolk on her plate; she wiped it up with a piece of toast. "Are we really going?"

"Yes."

"You promise?"

"Yes."

She kissed him and left a faint yellow stain on his cheek. "Where are we headed?"

"You'll find out."

"You won't tell me?"

"Nope. We're just going."

They finished breakfast. Eva piled the dishes in the sink, turned to go, thought about it for a second and decided to wash them. Buck went upstairs and got Eva's suitcase out of the closet where it was hidden. He got his own suitcase and filled it full of his stuff. He checked once around his room, once in the bath and once in Eva's bedroom for forgotten belongings. Then he picked up the two suitcases and carried them downstairs.

Eva was finishing up the dishes. He opened the front door and walked outside. The sunlight was so bright he could hardly see; then a cloud floated across the sun and cast everything in shadow. He walked down to his station wagon and piled the suitcases in through the rear window.

Eva appeared at the front door. She was holding a box of cookies, a paper bag full of apples and two feather pillows. She was smiling. She breathed deeply of the moist fresh air.

Buck walked up to her and put his hand on the door knob. "Is that it?"

"Yes," she said. "God, don't it smell good? I love it after it rains."

He shut the door firmly. He held her arm at the elbow and they walked to the car. Eva looked back at the house. "Goodbye, you dead house," she said. Then she got in the car.

Buck got in and started the motor. He let it warm up and then turned the car around in the muddy drive. Eva was all smiles. "I never felt so good," she said. Buck was beginning to feel pretty good himself. He was a little worried, about Ed, about everything, but that would pass. Everything always worked out. Anything was possible and nothing was inescapable; he was sure of that as he drove to the end of the driveway and looked up and down the empty highway.

As he pulled out and started heading north, the sun burst out of the clouds again and glittered brilliantly on the windshield of his car. He pressed the gas to the floor and they took off. The Pontiac waited a minute, two minutes, until the station wagon was only a bright speck receding in the distance. Then it pulled out of the oak trees and onto the highway. The sun glinted on its windshield as it accelerated silently. Its sleek blue body gleamed in the light, like a huge shark streaking through clear water.

Well, we have had a hard season hereabouts, let me
tell you; I can't remember a winter that was this mean,
ever. I don't mind a cold winter, you get one every
few years and no one can say why; the sky hangs like
a dead face and you expect it might snow, the air is
that cold and still, though of course it never does; we're
too low down for snow. But all the winter gardens get
froze out, and something draws back and dies inside the
ground; the juice, the blood, the kick, or whatever it

is that makes the crops come up, it gets discouraged, like a whipped dog; you can't make nothing grow in a soil that has lost its blood.

But like I said, I don't mind a cold winter, as long as there's plenty of rain. Our rain comes in off the Pacific, warm and soft; you can feel the tropical islands in it, all that green heat and steaminess. If you get enough of that rain, it will put the juice back in any soil; but this year we didn't get enough, not nearly. There wasn't but two weeks of it, and that was more like a cold drizzle than a tropical storm; then the sky dried up like a sick tit, the clouds broke up and it was all over, just like that. We are going to have trouble raising a decent crop of anything this year. It's only April, and the fields are dry as bone dust and the sky is that pure hot blue. You walk anywhere in the county, it feels like you're stepping on a corpse.

Noodles Pisco is dead and finally buried; I say finally cause there was some trouble over what to do with his body when it was found. Seems that once about ten years back when Noodles was strapped for cash he went and sold his body to medical science for eighty bucks; so when they had carted him down to the morgue in Stern there was a little fellow from the medical school already waiting, with a cold smile on his face and a slip of pink paper in his hand. It took old Armand Pisco a couple of days just to get possession of the corpse; he had to haggle with that little fellow, and threaten him, and show off the old Colt he always keeps tucked up in his belt; finally he slipped him two hundred dollars and the thing was settled. Then old Armand wouldn't have nothing to do with a funeral parlor, but had to go bury his son himself; it took six strong men just to get him out of the morgue, and another three or four to build a box and dig a hole big enough to lay him down in. From what I hear it got to be a mighty unpleasant business towards the end, what with the body all broken and swelled up, and parts of it smelly and burnt. They say two of the men fell over and fainted; Noodles would of got a laugh out of that, and been proud to know he done it. Anyhow, they finally got him planted—out on Armand's ranch up by Stimson Corners, on a rise beneath an oak.

There's been lots of wild talk over who it was killed Noodles. Of course the first thing that people figured was the Mexicans had done it, since they all hated Noodles and he hated them. And there was that time last spring, when a Mexican fellow got killed by Noodles and some others; it was an ugly affair, the sort that people don't forget. Well, for a couple of weeks everyone was sure it was the Mexicans, and some folks was getting ready to take revenge, getting themselves armed and organized and worked up; the Mexicans knew what was going on, of course, so it looked like there was going to be a regular war here in Royo County. But then all of a sudden County Sheriff Moon Cargo—you see, it was Moon took over after Noodles got it; nobody else was too eager, and Moon has always been the policeman type, sort of stocky and tough, with a thick blue jaw and a big round ass that sticks out like a flag— I say, Moon Cargo spoke up all of a sudden, and said it weren't the Mexicans, and he knew who had *really* done it. So we all said Who? And he said, Why that little creep Buck Goldberg, that was working for Leo

Train and shacking up with Ed Gray's wife. And we all said What? And he said, That's right, it's as plain as the egg on your face.

Moon's story is that the boy was a crook who came out to Yarbee to hide. Then he fell in with Eva, and he forced her to mess around; she was a good woman, but he beat her up or threatened her, or something, and since Ed Gray was out of town all the time she didn't have no one to protect her. But then Ed came home once, and caught them in the act; he tried to get rough, and the kid just up and killed him. Somehow or other Noodles found out; so the kid called in a few of his friends from the city, and they stomped old Noodles, and burned his car, and generally made it look like the Mexicans had done it. You ain't seen Ed Gray around lately, have you? Moon says. Or Eva, or that little creep that made her run away? No, he says, they're long gone; I just hope he don't do away with her too, when he gets tired of using her sweets.

Well, most everybody is going along with Moon now; he seems to know what he's talking about, and that thing about Buck and Eva makes good gossip. But I knew them, knew them both, so it appears to me that Moon's story is just a pile of hot crap. That boy wasn't any sort of a killer; he was a nice boy, honest and clean-cut. He was a little on the quiet side, but I like that; it shows he was interested in other folks. As for Eva, she was a fine woman, a good-looker and smart, too; she deserved a lot better than she got. If I was her and had to live with Ed Gray, all alone in that run-down Duggin house—which is who built it, and lived in it, and sold it; Doc Duggin, who was a vet, but who got rich taking the knife to girls in trouble, down in his musty basement—like I said, if I was Eva, I would of took off a long time ago, and found something that was better. But she stuck with Ed Gray, through all his trouble and all his mean moods. She wasn't any sort of a killer, no more than the boy was.

What really happened, is this: somehow or other, the boy got mixed up with a bunch of crooks back where he came from. He went along with them for a while, maybe he didn't know exactly what they was up to; but then he did some thinking, and he got scared, so he lit out for the countryside and tried to lay low. But the crooks wanted him back; maybe he knew too much already. So they got on his trail, and they traced him to Royo County. They drove in late at night, came in on highway seven. It might be they was speeding, or just looking suspicious; anyhow, they ran into Noodles Pisco, who was just coming home from Sacramento. Noodles pulled them over, and then something happened; maybe he saw a gun on one of them, or maybe they didn't have a license. So he got tough, but they were too quick; they got the draw on him and forced him off into the fields. They needed him dead, but they didn't want to use their guns, so they tied him up and stomped him, and then they burned his car. They made it look like a gang of Mexicans did it; it was easy for them, they was experts in death.

Now, what happened next I know for sure, because Leo Train saw it all, and he has told me the whole story. It was a little after sunrise, and Leo had just woke up when there was a knock on his door. He opened it and there was three big mean-looking colored fellows, and one of them was pointing a gun at his heart. They dragged him out in the street—it was broad daylight, but no one else was around—and one of the fellows held him while another one beat him up. Then they asked him where Buck was living, but he wouldn't talk; so they beat him some more, but he still wouldn't talk. Then they took their gun and put it up against his eyeball, and they said, Talk or die. So Leo told them, only he gave them the wrong directions; he sent them way out on highway seven, nearly all the way to Stimson Corners. Leo says he was scared to death; I think he did just fine.

Well, just purely by coincidence, purely by luck, Buck and Eva had decided that morning to pack up and run away together. Maybe someone tipped them off; maybe they just had a feeling, or maybe one of them had a dream that said, Get away now before it's too late. Whatever it was, they did it; they threw some clothes and such into Buck's old car and then they took off. The killers probably drove all the way to the county border before they figured out what was wrong; then they doubled back down highway seven. It might even be they passed Buck and Eva, going the other way; but they didn't notice, and when they finally found the house it was empty. Then they left the county as fast as they could; they knew Leo had fooled them, and they figured he would of called the state police.

Now that's what really happened. You can believe Moon Cargo if you want to, but I think he's all wet; or you can blame it all on the Mexicans, which is what folks have always done hereabouts. It's a free country, so take your choice: somebody's crazy, fancy story, or the real true facts, just like they happened. Believe me, I don't rightly care; it's all the same in my book. As for Ed Gray, who Moon says the boy killed in cold blood, I don't figure he's come to any harm at all. Ed is too mean, he's too low-down; he's the kind that never gets killed. Just for the fun of it I called up Navaho Truck, to see if they knew where he was. They said they didn't know and they didn't want to know; they fired him weeks ago, for driving like a maniac. What I think happened is, he got himself fired for something stupid, and he was so embarrassed he didn't dare come home. Who knows, maybe he was as tired of Eva as she was of him. You could tell they wasn't getting along, and sooner or later one of them was going to leave it.

Well, that's about it, I guess; that's all there is to tell. It's been a hard year all over the county, but we'll get on; the only thing I'm worried about is the ground. There's big cracks in it already, and it's just too dusty for April. Maybe we'll get some showers, it's been known to happen; a rain comes sometimes after everyone has given up, a really big wild rain that changes the whole picture. I wouldn't bet on it, but it could happen. If it don't there's going to be a lot of hungry and discouraged farmers hereabouts; I figure a lot of people will sell out this year. Let me tell you, it's a big temptation. Just this week there was a greasy-looking fellow in a big new Pontiac out at my place, waving a chunk of cash in my face; but I told him no, not this time. It would take a lot of money to get me off the farm; I don't know, I guess I like it. Maybe I'm just used to seeing flat; I need those flat fields stretching off all around me, lots of flat fields. This time of year there's a positive epidemic of wildflowers on them, millions of yellow flowers; they've sprouted up everywhere, even where it's dry and dusty. My daughter Pearl has figured out she's just another one of them yellow flowers; it's no use, she won't go to school, but spends all her time out rolling in the fields. I asked her what she was up to, but she wouldn't say; she just held her arms up around her head, and stood there perfectly still. Yesterday morning I followed her out a ways, thinking I would spy on her for a while. But she was wearing her yellow dress, and her hair is that soft shiny yellow; I swear she just disappeared, she melted right into that field of flowers.